YELLOWSTONE RISING

The Ground is Moving

A Psychological Thriller

By Faye Hollow

Published independently.

CONTENT WARNING

This novel contains scenes of natural disaster, injury, and life-threatening situations that may be distressing to some readers.

For those who listen

When the ground goes quiet.

THE LEGEND BENEATH YELLOWSTONE

Long before Yellowstone became a national park, long before boardwalks and guided tours, the land was already known.

Not as a destination.

As a warning.

Indigenous tribes of the region, including the Shoshone, Crow, and Blackfeet, understood Yellowstone as a place of power—one that was not meant to be disturbed without consequence. Stories passed through generations spoke of a land where the earth breathed, where the ground could open without warning, and where heat came from something deeper than fire.

Some traditions described Yellowstone as a place where the world beneath the surface pressed upward—restless, alive, and unpredictable—a place where balance mattered, and where disruption carried a cost.

Early explorers who entered the region told similar stories in different words. Reports described boiling earth, sudden eruptions, and animals behaving strangely before seismic events. Even without scientific language, the pattern was clear:

The land reacted.

Modern science confirms that Yellowstone sits above one of the largest volcanic systems on Earth. Beneath the park lies a vast network of magma, heat, and pressure—constantly shifting, constantly changing.

Most of the time, it releases that pressure slowly—through geysers, hot springs, and steam vents.

But not always.

This novel takes a simple question and pushes it further:

What happens when something interferes with that balance?

What happens when the system is no longer allowed to behave naturally?

And more importantly—

What happens when the land pushes back?

They said it was contained.

They said it was natural.

They were wrong.

Table of Contents

CHAPTER 1

The Talk

By ten in the morning, the boardwalk above the geyser basin was packed shoulder to shoulder with vacation hats, cameras, sunscreen, and the low, cheerful noise of people who had driven a long way to stand on top of something they barely believed was real.

Steam drifted across the mineral flats in white ribbons. Pools of hammered copper and bright poison-blue trembled under the sun. The air smelled of wet stone and sulfur and heat rising from somewhere old enough to ignore the difference between wonder and threat.

Ranger Cole Mercer walked backward at the head of the group, one hand lifted to keep a little boy from leaning too far over the rail.

"Hey, buddy. Unless you want to go home without eyebrows, stay on the boards."

A few adults laughed. The boy's mother grabbed the back of his shirt and smiled an embarrassed thank-you.

Cole turned, boots thudding softly on the planks, and kept moving. The boardwalk looped in a wide arc above the basin, the parking area a few hundred yards behind them, and nothing but unstable ground ahead.

He was broad-shouldered, sun-browned, and easy in his own body in the way men got after years outdoors. The flat brim of his ranger hat threw a clean line of shade across his face, but not enough to hide the confidence in it. He didn't have to perform authority. People just gave it to him.

On either side of the walkway, the basin hissed.

"This," he said, sweeping a hand toward the steaming ground, "is what happens when Yellowstone decides not to be subtle."

A few phones came up.

He gave them a grin that landed well with tourists because it made the place feel both grand and manageable, which was exactly the trick.

"You're standing on one of the largest active volcanic systems in the world. No, that does not mean it's about to blow today, so let's keep everyone's blood pressure down. What it does mean is that the earth under your feet is thin, hot, and full of water trying very hard to become steam."

He tapped the boardwalk rail with two knuckles.

"That's why you stay on these. Ground that looks solid out here can break like pie crust. And what's underneath it is hot enough to ruin your whole summer."

That got a bigger laugh.

A man near the back, with expensive sunglasses and a camera hanging from his neck, raised a hand. "So the supervolcano thing—that's real?"

Cole nodded. "Real enough. The whole park sits over a giant magma system. But Yellowstone has always been Yellowstone. Geysers, hot springs, mud pots, steam vents—that's the heartbeat here."

A girl, maybe twelve years old, frowned up at him. "Heartbeat?"

He slowed, letting the group bunch naturally around him as a plume of steam rolled across the path and thinned again.

"Yeah. The park talks. You learn to listen."

He said it lightly, but the words stuck in his own ears harder than usual.

The basin fell off. Not quite unbalanced. Like the ground had shifted a fraction out of rhythm with itself, something underneath it pushing harder than it should.

Not dramatic. Not obvious. Just wrong in the way a room could feel wrong when someone stopped talking the second you opened the door.

He kept walking.

To the west, beyond a stretch of mineral crust and low steam, a herd of bison stood on the rise above the basin road.

They were too still. Cole had seen it once before, years ago—horses refusing a trail before a quake no one else felt yet. Animals didn't wait for explanations. They moved on pressure, on vibration, on something deeper than sound.

Cole's eyes flicked to them, then back to the group.

"Now, if you see wildlife, remember two things. One, this is their home. Two, they can absolutely wreck yours."

A couple of people laughed again, but he wasn't really with them anymore.

There were maybe twenty bison on the hill: big dark bodies, blocky heads, humps like old muscle under shaggy fur. Not grazing, not drifting, just standing shoulder to shoulder, facing the basin.

Watching.

He slowed enough that the woman nearest him almost walked into his back.

"Sorry," she said.

Cole lifted a hand without turning. "You're fine."

He looked harder.

No calves moving between legs. No tails flicking. No lazy angle to them. Their stillness had a shape to it—a pressure.

One of the older men in the group noticed where he was looking. "Bison?"

Cole gave a distracted nod. "Yeah."

“Can we get closer?”

“No.”

The answer came out sharp enough that several heads turned.

Cole softened it a second later. “No, sir. They’re unpredictable on a good day. And they weigh as much as a small car.”

The man chuckled, but it died when Cole didn’t.

A breeze crossed the basin, carrying heat against his face. He heard the usual sounds—the hiss of vents, the mutter of tourists, a camera shutter clicking three times in a row.

Then something dropped out of the world.

Cole stopped.

The girl who had asked about the heartbeat nearly bumped him and caught herself on the rail.

“What is it?”

He didn’t answer.

No birds.

He hadn’t even noticed them until they weren’t there. A few ravens earlier. Some swallows are cutting across the stream—songbirds in the scrub beyond the basin. Yellowstone always had layers of sound if you knew how to separate them.

Now the sky above the basin had gone clean and empty.

No flicker. No wingbeat. Nothing.

A man near the middle of the group lifted his phone toward a geyser pool. “Is there usually this much steam?”

Cole looked up.

His voice came back lower. "Everybody stay on the boardwalk."

The cheerful vacation murmur faded. People heard the change before they understood it.

A little girl in a pink windbreaker said, "Mom?"

Cole stepped to the rail and looked again at the bison.

Still staring.

Then one of them shifted. Not grazing, not turning away. Just planted one front hoof and snorted hard enough that vapor burst from its nostrils.

Another did the same.

Then a third.

Cole's skin tightened across his shoulders.

He pulled the radio from his vest. "Mercer to Basin Station."

Static cracked, then a bored voice. "Go ahead, Mercer."

Cole kept his eyes on the ridge. "You seeing the herd above Grand Prism access?"

A pause. "Negative. Why?"

He didn't take his eyes off them. "I've got twenty, maybe more. Not moving right. Alert road patrol and get somebody to—"

The boardwalk gave a tiny shiver under his boots.

Not a tremor. Not really. More like the ground had flexed and thought better of it. Not release—resistance. Like pressure building, then stopping short of breaking through.

Several tourists felt it at once. A few gasped. One woman laughed nervously and looked around for everyone else to confirm she wasn't crazy.

"You feel that?" someone said.

Cole did not answer the radio.

He crouched and pressed two fingers to the warm planks.

Another vibration came up through the wood. Light. Fast. Wrong.

His jaw locked.

"Mercer?" the radio voice said, louder now. "What's going on?"

Cole stood in one motion and turned to the group.

"Everybody listen to me."

The easy tour-guide warmth was gone. What replaced it moved faster.

"I need you all to stay calm and start heading back the way we came. No running. Stay together. Parents, keep your kids close. Right now."

Questions hit him immediately.

"Why?"

"What happened?"

"Is this an earthquake?"

Cole pointed down the boardwalk. "Move."

That did it.

People started turning, gathering children, adjusting backpacks, fumbling with cameras. Shoes knocked on the boards in a clumsy, rising rhythm. The little crowd folded back on itself, uncertain but obedient.

Cole stayed where he was, watching the ridge.

The herd moved all at once. No warning. No hesitation.

Not a graze. Not even shuffling.

A surge.

Massive heads dropped. Hooves tore at the ground. Dirt kicked up behind them in a brown wave as the bison launched downhill toward the basin road.

Toward the people.

Cole's voice ripped across the steam.

"Run!"

CHAPTER 2

Stampede

The word hit a half-second too late.

Hooves pounding. Not scattered. Not even hesitant. A rolling surge that swallowed everything else—the hiss of steam, the chatter of people, even the sharp crack of someone dropping a phone onto the boardwalk.

"Move!" Cole barked, already turning, already shoving bodies into motion. They were still heading back toward the main access trail—the only solid route out of the basin.

The herd broke the ridge like a collapsing wall. Straight downhill—cutting across the road and driving directly toward the boardwalk. Dirt and rock sprayed behind them as the bison barreled downhill, heads low, shoulders driving, a wave of muscle and bone aimed straight at the basin road.

Toward the boardwalk.

“Go!” Cole grabbed the nearest man by the strap of his backpack and yanked him forward. “Don’t stop—keep moving!”

Panic snapped through the group. Order dissolved. People shoved, stumbled, grabbed for kids, for each other, for anything.

A woman froze in the middle of the path, eyes locked on the charging animals.

Cole hit her shoulder hard enough to spin her. “Run!”

She moved.

The ground shivered again under his boots—harder this time. The planks rattled, a loose vibration that didn’t belong.

Someone screamed.

Cole spun.

A boy had tripped near the rail, knees skidding across the wood, his hands scrambling for grip. His mother was already reaching for him, but the surge of bodies shoved her past him.

Cole lunged, dropping low, one hand hooking the back of the kid’s jacket. He hauled him up and shoved him forward into his mother’s arms.

“Don’t let go of him!”

“I won’t—thank you—”

“No stopping!”

He turned again.

The first bison hit the road.

It didn’t slow. Didn’t hesitate. It crossed the asphalt in a blur of dark mass and flying dirt, then slammed into the edge of the basin, hooves tearing into the mineral crust as it drove forward.

Another followed. Then another.

They weren't spreading out.

They were coming straight through.

"Off the main path!" Cole shouted. "Move to the pullouts—give them space!"

A man tried to run against the flow, dragging a rolling suitcase behind him like he was still in an airport.

"Drop it!" Cole yelled.

The man hesitated—just long enough.

A bison veered, clipped him with the full force of its shoulder, and the man disappeared under it.

The suitcase burst open, clothes whipping into the air. Cole didn't look back—but he already knew. There was no getting up from that. No space in the surge for survival.

The sound that came out of the crowd wasn't a scream. It was something raw. Animal.

Cole didn't look down. He didn't stop.

"Keep moving!" he roared, driving the group forward with both arms, shoving, pulling, forcing momentum back into people who wanted to freeze.

A second surge of bison hit the boardwalk edge.

One of them slipped on the wood, hooves skidding, and slammed sideways into the rail. The wood cracked. The rail snapped outward, and the animal half-fell, half-lunged onto the planks.

People scattered.

"Off! Off the boards!" Cole grabbed a teenage girl by the wrist and dragged her clear as the bison's back leg kicked, catching another tourist in the thigh and throwing him into the dirt.

Steam rolled up around them, thick and blinding.

The air stung his throat.

Cole shoved the girl toward a patch of open ground. "Stay down!"

He pivoted, scanning.

Bodies everywhere. Some moving. Some not.

"Ranger!" someone screamed. "Help—please—"

Cole locked onto the voice.

A woman lay twisted near the edge of a shallow thermal pool, one leg bent wrong, her hand clawing at the ground as she tried to drag herself away from the water.

The pool's surface trembled, heat rippling across it.

Cole sprinted.

A bison thundered past behind him, close enough that the air punched against his back. He didn't break stride.

He dropped beside the woman, grabbed her under the arms. "I've got you—don't fight me."

"It's—my leg—"

"I know."

He hauled her back, muscles burning, boots slipping on the wet mineral crust. The ground felt soft under him.

"Hold on," he muttered.

Another tremor rippled through the basin.

The pool beside them burped—water lifting, sloshing, then settling again with a hiss.

Cole dragged her another few feet, then another, until they cleared the edge.

"Stay here," he said, lowering her gently. "Don't move."

"I can't—"

"I know."

He stood, already turning.

The herd was still moving, but the first wave had passed. Dust hung in the air. Steam curled through it, turning everything hazy.

People were scattered across the basin, some crouched low, some screaming, some just staring.

"Listen to me!" Cole shouted, stepping up onto a broken section of boardwalk. "Everyone who can walk—move to me. Now!"

It took a second.

Then another.

Then they started coming.

Slow at first. Then faster. Limping, crying, clutching each other. A man with blood running down his face. A woman barefoot, one shoe gone. A kid sobbing into his own hands.

Cole pointed toward the main access trail. "We're getting out of this basin. Stay together. Nobody goes alone."

"Is it over?" someone asked.

Cole didn't answer.

Because the ground under his boots was still wrong.

He keyed his radio, breath tight but controlled. "Basin Station, this is Ranger Mercer. We have multiple injuries, at least one fatal. Bison stampede—aggressive behavior, not defensive. I need medical response now."

Static.

Then the same bored voice, thinner now. "Copy the injuries. Bison incidents happen, Mercer. Keep your people calm and—"

"This wasn't an incident," Cole snapped. "They came through like they were being pushed. I need—"

"Negative on escalation," the voice cut in. "We're logging it as animal agitation. Response teams are en route. Stay within protocol."

Cole stared at the radio as it had just insulted him.

"Protocol?" he said. "You didn't see what just—"

"Stay within protocol, Ranger."

The line went dead.

Cole lowered the radio slowly.

Around him, people were still moving, still breathing, still alive because they'd gotten lucky.

He turned back toward the ridge.

The herd was gone.

Not scattered.

Gone.

The sky above the basin was still empty. Then, faint at first, a single bird cut across the horizon. Then another. Not a return to normal—just enough to say the ground wasn't screaming at them the way it had before.

No birds. No sound but the distant hiss of steam and the ragged breathing of the survivors behind him.

Cole's jaw tightened.

They hadn't been charging for food.

Or territory.

Or fear of people.

They had been running from something. Not predators. Not people. From the ground itself—something pushing up beneath their hooves, something they could feel long before humans could.

And whatever it was—

It was still out there.

CHAPTER 3

First Blast

Cole moved fast along the boardwalk, boots hitting hard, the air still thick with the aftermath of the stampede—dust hanging low, steam drifting sideways in uneven sheets. The place looked scraped raw.

"Basin Station, Mercer," he said into the radio as he walked. "I'm heading back to the incident site."

A pause. Then, flat: "Copy. Medical teams are inbound. Stay clear if possible."

Cole didn't answer.

He stepped off the main flow of people and cut toward the edge of the geyser basin, eyes scanning the ground, the pools, the vents. He wasn't looking for blood.

He was looking for what had set the animals off.

The boardwalk creaked under him as he crossed a narrow stretch over pale, cracked earth. Steam hissed out of a vent to his right, louder than it should have been. The sound rose, fell, then rose again.

He slowed.

A cluster of tourists lingered ahead despite the chaos, drawn back in the way people always were. Phones up. Voices low, excited, shaky.

"Hey," Cole called. "You need to move back—"

Someone laughed nervously. "It's fine, it's just a geyser—"

Cole's eyes snapped to the pool beside them.

The water wasn't right. Pressure spikes didn't look like this—not unless something below was forcing water upward faster than the system could release it.

It wasn't the usual rolling simmer. It pulsed. The surface domed slightly, then dropped. Domed again.

"Back!" Cole barked, already moving. "Get back now!"

They turned too slowly.

The ground shuddered under his feet—hard enough this time that the boardwalk rattled.

The pool swelled. Right beside the boardwalk—less than ten feet from where the tourists had been standing.

Then it detonated. The plume collapsed outward…

The blast rose and burst into a violent roar, a column of boiling water and steam ripping into the air. It hit—heat, force, noise—throwing Cole sideways as the shockwave tore across the basin.

People screamed.

The plume collapsed outward, scalding water raining down in a wide arc. Steam slammed into the boardwalk, blinding white, burning hot.

Cole hit the planks, shoulder first, breath punched out of him.

"Down!" he shouted, dragging himself up. "Get down!"

A man staggered past him, clutching his face, skin already reddening, blistering.

"Help—help—"

"On the ground!" Cole grabbed him, shoved him flat. "Stay down!"

Another scream cut through the steam.

Higher. Sharper.

Cole turned toward it, squinting through the white haze. Shapes moved—people running blind, slipping, colliding.

The air burned his throat.

"Move away from the water!" he yelled. "Away from the basin!"

The ground trembled again, a rapid, jittering vibration that rattled through his legs.

"Ranger!" someone screamed. "Please—"

Cole locked onto the voice.

A woman lay near the edge of the pool, half on the boardwalk, half off it. Steam curled around her legs. Her hands clawed at the wood, trying to pull herself away.

The pool surged again beside her, water sloshing over the edge in a boiling sheet. It wasn't cycling—it was being forced. Each surge was stronger than the last, as if something below were driving it upward faster than it could release.

Cole ran.

Heat slammed into him as he closed the distance. The air felt thick and wet. He dropped low, grabbed her under the arms.

"I've got you—don't fight me."

"It's burning—oh God—"

"I know."

He hauled her back, boots slipping on the wet planks. The wood hissed where the water hit it, droplets popping, jumping.

Another surge from the pool.

Cole yanked harder, dragging her clear just as a fresh wave of boiling water splashed over the edge where she'd been.

It hit the boardwalk with a violent hiss.

He pulled her another few feet, then another, until the heat eased just enough to breathe.

"Stay with me," he said, lowering her onto the planks. "Stay with me."

Her skin was already mottling red, patches turning white.

"Don't—don't leave—"

"I'm right here."

He looked up.

The basin was a mess of movement and noise. People scattering, some dropping to the ground, others running in the wrong direction. Steam still rolled in thick waves, hiding half the scene.

"Everyone back!" Cole shouted, pushing to his feet. "Get off the boardwalk—move to open ground!"

A man stumbled toward him, eyes wide. "What was that?"

Cole didn't answer.

Because the pool wasn't settling.

It churned. Violent, unstable. The surface buckled as if something underneath it were trying to get out.

Another tremor hit—short, sharp.

The boardwalk shivered.

Cole grabbed his radio, breath tight. "Basin Station, Mercer—this was not a normal eruption. I repeat, not normal. I've got multiple burn victims, unstable ground, and—"

Static cracked over his words.

Then: "Copy the injuries. Hydrothermal events occur—"

"No," Cole snapped, eyes locked on the pool. "This isn't—this isn't a cycle. It's a building. Something's pushing it."

A pause.

Then, colder: "Stay within protocol, Ranger. Medical is en route."

Cole stared at the radio.

"Protocol?" he said under his breath.

Behind him, the woman groaned, trying to move.

"Don't," he said, crouching again, steadying her. "Just breathe. Help's coming."

She nodded weakly, teeth clenched.

Cole looked back at the pool.

It surged again—too fast, too irregular.

Geysers didn't behave like this.

They didn't explode without warning, then keep building.

They didn't feel like they were about to tear the ground apart.

Cole rose slowly, scanning the basin, the vents, the cracks in the pale earth that seemed just a little wider than they had been an hour ago.

The air tightened. The ground thinned.

This wasn't a one-off. It was stepping outward—one basin, then the next—like pressure searching for the weakest place to break through.

And whatever had driven the animals out—

It hadn't passed.

It was getting closer. The ground held—for now—but the heat was still there, deep and waiting, like something that hadn't decided yet whether it was finished.

CHAPTER 4

The Agent Arrives

By the time the first medical chopper cut across the sky, Yellowstone no longer looked like a park.

It felt occupied.

Cole stood at the edge of the basin with burned tourists lying out on jackets and backpacks behind him, each one watched over by somebody pale and shaking. Sirens wailed in bursts from the access road. Park medics rushed in, then slowed when they saw the ground still steaming and the shattered stretch of boardwalk hanging half-broken over the mineral crust.

Then the black vehicles came.

Not park service trucks. Not a county response.

Three matte SUVs rolled past the medical staging area without hesitation, tires hissing on the hot pavement, windows dark enough to turn the people inside into silhouettes. Another followed behind them, pulling a trailer loaded with equipment under gray tarps.

They moved too fast for confusion.

A paramedic near Cole muttered, “Who the hell are they?”

Cole didn’t answer. He was watching the convoy spread out with practiced precision—one vehicle angling toward the basin road, another cutting across the turnout, the third stopping between the tourists and the shattered boardwalk as somebody had already planned exactly where the lines would be drawn.

Doors opened.

Men in windbreakers stepped out first. No park insignia. No county patches. They moved with clipped efficiency, talking into earpieces, scanning faces, pointing people away from the basin as if they owned the ground.

Cole took two steps forward.

A medic caught his arm. “Cole—”

He pulled free. “No.”

One of the SUVs’ rear doors opened last.

The man who stepped out didn’t look like a field operator. He looked like somebody who should’ve been in a secure office three states away, controlling screens and bad outcomes from behind glass.

Tall. Lean. Dark jacket zipped to the throat. No hat. No visible rush in him at all.

His hair was trimmed too neatly for the wind ripping across the basin. His face was narrow, pale, unreadable. Wire-frame glasses sat on a nose that looked as if it had never been broken, which, in Cole's experience, usually meant the man either avoided physical problems for a living or paid other people to absorb them.

He took one look at the basin and not much changed in his expression.

A woman with blistered hands cried out as paramedics shifted her onto a stretcher. The man glanced at her, then at the broken boardwalk, then at the steaming pool that had erupted.

Not rattled. Just measuring.

Cole met him halfway.

"This area's unstable," Cole said. "You need to stay off the boards."

The man stopped just inside Cole's space and took him in from hat to boots, not intimidated, not impressed.

"Ranger Mercer."

Not a question.

Cole's eyes narrowed. "And you are?"

The man reached into his jacket, produced a credential wallet, and flashed it just long enough to be more of an insult than information.

"Elias Voss."

Cole caught a seal, an eagle, a line of print, then it was gone.

"That supposed to mean something to me?"

"No," Voss said. His voice was even, precise, almost dry. "It isn't."

Behind him, his people were already moving.

One team unrolled yellow barriers and began blocking the main walkway—another redirected medics to a new perimeter farther back from the basin. A third started photographing the ground, the vents, the broken rail, each position taken with the speed of a drill they'd practiced before.

Cole turned, disbelief sharpening into anger. "Who authorized this?"

Voss didn't look where Cole was looking. "This area is now under federal containment." Emergency authority. Pre-cleared, pre-signed. The kind that didn't wait for permission once certain thresholds were crossed.

"Containment for what?"

"For an active geothermal hazard."

"That's my call to make on this basin."

"It was," Voss said.

Cole stepped closer. "People got burned because something down there blew without warning, and now you show up with a convoy and start fencing off a national park like you've been waiting for it."

Voss's gaze settled on him. Cool. Unblinking. Clinical in a way that felt less like calm and more like a dissection.

"You made multiple radio reports," he said. "Abnormal animal behavior. Ground vibration. Irregular hydrothermal activity. Then a public casualty event."

Cole stared at him.

He'd heard the reports.

All of them.

"You got here fast," Cole said. They'd been waiting for it. Too fast for coincidence. Like they hadn't responded to the event—

"We were already in the region." Waiting.

"Doing what?"

Voss ignored the question. "How many witnesses directly observed the pool behavior before the blast?"

Cole let out a short laugh with no humor in it. "That's what matters to you?"

"It matters now."

A helicopter thundered overhead, forcing both men to glance up. Dust and steam kicked sideways under the rotor wash. One of the burned tourists started screaming again as medics tried to load him.

Cole pointed toward the stretchers. "What matters is them."

Voss looked over. "They're being treated."

"They're being treated because I pulled them out."

A beat passed.

Not tension. Just a calculation.

Then Voss said, "Walk me through the sequence."

Cole did not move. "You first. Who are your people?"

"Federal response."

"That's not an answer."

"It's the one you're getting."

Cole's jaw tightened hard enough to ache.

Voss nodded once toward the basin. "The sequence, Ranger."

Cole should have told him to go to hell.

Instead, because injured people were still being loaded behind him and the ground was still wrong under his boots, he gave the short version—the bison. The birds are disappearing—the first vibration. The tourists linger. The way the pool had pulsed instead of cycling.

Voss listened without interrupting, one hand lightly touching the edge of his glasses as if pinning a thought in place. Not once did he ask Cole to clarify the basics. Not once did he look surprised.

When Cole finished, Voss's eyes shifted briefly to the unstable pool.

"You're certain the birds vanished before the first blast?"

Cole caught that. "That's the part you care about?"

"It's the part I asked about."

"Yes," Cole said. "Mid-sentence. Sky went empty."

Something flickered behind Voss's eyes. Recognition.

Gone just as fast.

Cole saw it anyway.

"You already knew," he said.

"No."

"That's a lie." Cole didn't soften it.

Voss adjusted one cuff with irritating calm. "It's an incomplete statement."

Cole took a step toward him. "Try the complete one."

Two of Voss's men looked over immediately. They didn't move yet, but they were ready.

Voss noticed that too and gave the slightest shake of his head. Stand down.

Then he looked back at Cole. "What I know," he said, "is that panic spreads faster than steam. So from this point on, you will direct your staff to refer all questions, all statements, and all incident reports to my team."

Cole just stared at him. "No."

"This isn't a negotiation."

"It's my park."

"And this is now my scene."

A fresh line of barriers snapped into place behind them. Tourists were being herded farther back, phones lowered by men who had no legal right, Cole could see, to touch them, yet were doing it anyway.

One of the park medics jogged up, face flushed. "Cole, they're shutting the south access. They told us no one goes past the lot without—"

Voss didn't even turn. "That's correct."

The medic looked between them. "Who is this?"

Cole answered without taking his eyes off Voss. "That's what I'm trying to find out."

Voss finally glanced at the medic. "Move the injured. No one else enters the basin."

"We still have rangers unaccounted for on the west trail," the medic said.

"Then call them out."

"There's a family still asking for their son—"

"Call. Them. Out."

The medic looked at Cole.

Cole said, "Go help the injured. I'll deal with this."

The medic hesitated, then backed off.

Voss waited until he was gone. "You need to understand the scale of what you're interfering with."

Cole let that sit.

Then: "There it is."

Voss didn't blink. "There, what is?"

"The part where you admit this didn't surprise you."

A hard silence opened between them. Steam drifted through it.

Finally, Voss said, "What happened here will be classified as a localized hydrothermal instability event. That is the language that will be used."

Cole laughed once. "Localized."

"Yes."

"You had bison stampeding through tourists and a basin that blew like a pipe bomb."

"Localized, Yellowstone was always under pressure," Voss said. "But it was stable—contained by its own systems. What your people did—what we did—was tap into it, redirect it, force it to move faster than it ever would have on its own." Evacuation had already pushed miles beyond the basin—farther than anyone on camera was being told.

Cole took one step closer until Voss had to tip his chin slightly up to keep eye contact. “Listen to me carefully. Animals don’t run downhill into crowds for fun. Birds don’t vanish in the middle of the day because a pool feels moody. Something is driving this.”

Voss held his gaze. “Then leave the analysis to people equipped to do it.”

Cole’s mouth flattened. “You mean people are already hiding it?”

A voice crackled in Voss’s earpiece. Low. Urgent.

Voss turned his head enough to listen, then faced Cole again.

“Your access is revoked,” he said.

Cole thought he’d misheard him. “What?”

“Effective immediately. You are relieved of field duty in the basin and adjacent sectors pending federal review.”

“You can’t do that.”

“I just did.”

Cole’s laugh came back sharper this time. “I’m not one of your people.”

“No,” Voss said. “You’re the reason I’m here.”

Cole moved before he thought better of it, grabbing a fistful of Voss’s jacket and slamming him back against the side of the SUV hard enough to make the door shudder.

Every nearby federal body snapped toward them.

“Tell me what you’re doing in my park,” Cole said.

Voss's glasses stayed on somehow, making the moment stranger.

He looked down once at Cole's fist, then back up at Cole's face. Still maddeningly composed. Still not afraid enough.

"Common sense," Voss said quietly, "would suggest this is the part where you let go."

Cole tightened his grip.

A half-circle of armed federal personnel closed in.

Boots on gravel. Hands near jackets. Controlled, but close.

Voss spoke without looking at them. "Stand by."

Nobody touched Cole.

That meant Voss still wanted something.

Cole leaned in. "You want my reports? Here's one. This place is getting worse by the minute, and you're wasting time playing cleanup."

Voss's voice dropped lower. "And you're confusing access with understanding."

Then, after a beat:

"You are done here, Ranger."

Cole let go with a hard shove.

Voss straightened his jacket as if nothing had happened. He looked toward the basin, toward the steam still rising in jagged bursts beyond the broken rail.

Then he gave the order that changed everything.

"Escort Ranger Mercer off-site," he said. "His authority in Yellowstone is suspended until further notice."

Cole stared at him.

Around them, men moved. Not fast. Not sloppy. Like they'd expected this too. Like he was already paperwork in their heads.

For the first time that day, something colder than anger slid under his skin.

Not fear.

Recognition.

Whatever was happening under Yellowstone—

It was bigger than the blast.

And the people now controlling the park had no intention of letting him anywhere near it again.

CHAPTER 5

Controlled Narrative

By late afternoon, Yellowstone didn't look like itself anymore.

Roadblocks went up first—portable barriers dragged into place across access roads, orange cones snapping into neat lines that funneled traffic away from the basin. Park rangers who had worked the same routes for years were redirected like tourists, waved off by men with no uniforms and no patience.

Cole stood just outside the perimeter, watching it happen.

"Sir, you can't stand here."

He didn't move.

A young federal officer—too clean boots, too stiff posture—gestured toward the parking lot behind him. "We need you to clear the area."

"I work here."

"Not right now, you don't."

Cole turned his head slowly and looked at him.

The officer held it for about two seconds, then glanced away first.

"Move back, sir," he said, quieter now.

Cole stepped past him anyway.

No one grabbed him.

Not yet.

The basin was half-visible through drifting steam and the bodies moving in controlled lines across it. Equipment had been brought in fast—tripods, sensors, cables unspooling across the ground like someone was wiring the place for something bigger than a one-off incident.

Two men lifted a section of broken boardwalk and set it aside like debris that didn't matter anymore.

Cole spotted a cluster of media vans at the far edge of the lot, their satellite dishes rising like metal flowers above the crowd. A reporter stood in front of a camera, hair pinned in place despite the wind, voice steady despite what had happened here.

"…minor hydrothermal disturbance earlier today," she said, eyes locked on the lens. "Park officials confirm that injuries were limited, and there is no ongoing threat to visitors."

Behind her, a stretcher rolled past with a man whose arms were wrapped in gauze thick enough to hide the damage underneath.

"Limited," Cole muttered.

A second reporter stepped in beside her, nodding along. "Authorities are calling it an isolated event. Officials are urging calm and encouraging visitors to continue enjoying the park safely."

He turned away before he did something that would make this worse.

A line of park staff stood off to one side, clustered together, watching the same thing he was. People he knew. People who had worked this land long enough to know when something was off.

One of them, a woman named Harris, caught his eye. "You okay?"

"No," Cole said.

She nodded once. "Yeah."

"What are they telling you?"

"Same as everyone else. Keep people calm. Stay out of the basin. Let the federal government handle it."

Cole glanced back toward the controlled chaos. "Does that sit right with you?"

Harris shook her head. "Nothing about today sits right."

A truck rolled past them—unmarked, matte black, tires crunching over gravel. It didn't slow or signal. Just cut across the lot and head for a narrow service road that leads away from the main tourist areas.

Toward restricted terrain.

Cole watched it go.

Another followed. Then a third.

"What's out there?" Harris asked, following his gaze.

"Nothing tourists ever see," Cole said.

The third vehicle disappeared into the trees.

Cole's jaw tightened.

"They're not leaving," he said.

Harris frowned. "What?"

"They're not here to shut this down," Cole said. "They're going deeper."

A shout broke across the lot.

"Hey—stay behind the barrier!"

Cole turned.

A family tried to duck under the tape line, the father arguing, pointing toward the basin. "My son was over there—someone said—"

A federal officer stepped in front of him, firm, unyielding. "Sir, you need to step back."

"I need to know where my kid is—"

"You'll be informed through proper channels."

"Proper—are you kidding me?"

The officer didn't move.

Didn't blink.

Cole stepped forward before he thought about it.

"Let me talk to him," he said.

The officer shook his head. "Orders."

Cole leaned in just enough. "You don't know this ground. I do."

The officer's jaw tightened. "Orders."

Cole held his stare for a second longer, then stepped back.

The father's voice cracked behind him. "Please—"

Cole didn't look back.

Information in. Nothing out.

A low vibration rolled under his boots.

Stronger this time.

Not sharp like the last ones—heavier.

Cole stilled.

Harris felt it too. "You feel that?"

"Yeah."

The gravel at their feet shifted, a faint, uneven ripple, as if something were moving far below the surface.

A nearby cone tipped slightly, then settled.

One of the federal agents glanced down, then away, as he'd already decided it didn't matter.

Cole looked toward the basin.

Steam pulsed in irregular bursts, not the steady exhale it should have been. The air shimmered with heat, but underneath it—something else.

Presssure building..

Another tremor hit, short and hard enough to make a few people stumble.

Someone laughed nervously. "Aftershocks, right?"

No one answered.

Cole's eyes tracked back to the service road.

The last of the unmarked vehicles had vanished into the trees.

They weren't responding. They weren't evacuating. They were working.

He stepped back from the perimeter.

"Where are you going?" Harris asked.

Cole didn't stop. "To find out what they're doing."

"You just got pulled off duty."

"Yeah," Cole said.

Another tremor rolled through the ground, deeper this time, the kind that settled in your bones instead of just your feet.

He kept walking.

"That doesn't change anything."

Behind him, the park continued to reshape itself into something quieter.

Controlled.

Managed.

A version of Yellowstone that didn't match what was happening underneath it.

Cole didn't look back.

Whatever had pushed the animals out…

Whatever had blown that basin apart…

It wasn't finished.

And the people now in charge weren't trying to stop it.

They were hiding it.

Cole broke into a jog as he hit the edge of the lot and cut toward the trees, following the route the unmarked vehicles had taken.

The ground shuddered again under his stride.

Stronger.

Closer.

He didn't slow.

If they thought he was going to stand down—

They didn't know him at all.

CHAPTER 6

Off the Map

Cole left the pavement behind and cut into the trees at a run.

The service road wasn't meant for visitors—just a narrow strip of packed dirt winding through lodgepole pine, half-hidden by brush and the kind of neglect that kept people from asking questions. Tire tracks cut deep into the dust, fresh and sharp-edged.

He followed them.

Branches snapped against his shoulders. Pine needles crushed under his boots. The air smelled cleaner here—less sulfur, more earth—but it wasn't safer.

Another tremor rolled underfoot.

Short and heavy. Closer.

Cole slowed just enough to listen.

No tourists. No voices. Just wind threading through the trees and something else—low and mechanical.

He moved again, angling downhill toward the tracks.

The road bent around a rise, then dropped into a shallow clearing.

Cole stopped.

Two rigs stood in the open ground—tall, skeletal structures braced with steel supports, cables running down into the earth through reinforced collars that had been drilled straight through the crust. Portable generators thudded nearby, their engines vibrating through the ground in a steady pulse.

Men moved between them in hard hats and dark jackets, not uniforms, Cole recognized. No insignia.

One of the rigs let out a sharp metallic whine.

Cole stepped off the road and into the brush, lowering himself behind a line of fallen timber.

A worker adjusted a control panel mounted to the side of the nearest rig. Numbers flickered across a small screen—too far away to read, but the man's posture was tight, focused.

Another shouted over the engine noise. "Pressure's climbing again—"

"Hold it," someone snapped. "Hold it—don't vent yet."

Cole's jaw tightened.

The second rig shuddered, then steadied.

A pipe running from its base jerked slightly, as something inside it had just forced its way upward and been pushed back down.

This wasn't monitoring.

Cole shifted his position, crawling along the fallen logs until he had a better angle.

The ground around the rigs didn't look right.

The pale crust had been broken open in a wide circle, reinforced with metal plates and bolted seams. Steam leaked from the edges in thin, constant threads. The earth beneath it seemed thinner.

Another tremor hit.

This one made the rig sway.

A man grabbed the frame to steady himself. "We're losing stability!"

"Then compensate!" came the answer. "We don't shut down."

Cole's gaze followed the pipe.

It ran from the rig into a larger system set farther back—something bulkier, more complex.

He edged forward again, careful, slow.

Branches brushed his sleeves. Dirt smeared across his palms.

Then he saw it.

A cluster of reinforced valves connected to a thick central conduit driven deep into the ground. The metal was scorched in places, with heat discoloration spreading outward from the joints.

One of the valves shuddered.

Then snapped open.

A blast of steam tore out with a violent hiss, venting upward in a white column that twisted through the trees.

The sound punched through the clearing.

Men flinched.

One swore. “That’s too much—”

“Close it!” another yelled. “Close it now!”

The valve slammed shut.

The pipe rattled.

The ground beneath it trembled again—harder.

Cole felt it through his chest.

He looked back toward the rigs.

Toward the basin.

Toward the direction the stampede had come from.

His stomach dropped.

Another worker ran toward the second rig. “We’re getting feedback from the west basin—”

“Ignore it,” someone barked. “Stay on target.”

Stay on target.

Cole’s grip tightened on the log beneath him.

A loud crack split the air.

Cole’s head snapped toward the sound.

One of the support braces on the second rig jerked, then settled again.

A man swore under his breath. “We’re pushing too hard—”
They weren’t just drilling—they were pulling heat and pressure out of one zone and forcing it into another, trying to keep the system stable long enough to reach whatever they’d found below.

“We don’t have a choice,” came the reply.

Cole shifted his weight.

A branch snapped under his knee.

The sound was small.

In the clearing, everything paused.

One of the men turned.

Not fully.

Just enough.

Cole froze.

The man's head tilted slightly, eyes scanning the tree line.

Not alarmed—aware.

Cole didn't move.

Didn't breathe.

The man took one step forward.

Then another.

Slow.

Deliberate.

Watching.

Cole's pulse thudded in his ears.

The man's gaze slid past him—

Then stopped.

Locked.

Cole saw it.

The man didn't shout.

Didn't reach for a radio.

He just raised one hand slightly, signaling to someone out of view.

And smiled, just a little.

CHAPTER 7

Containment Attempt

The man didn't call out.

He didn't need to.

Two figures stepped out from behind the second rig like they'd been standing there the whole time, just out of sight—dark jackets. No insignia. Hands loose at their sides, but ready.

Cole moved first.

He pushed off the log and broke left, crashing through brush before the first shout could catch up to him.

"Hey—!"

Too late.

Branches whipped across his face. Pine needles exploded under his boots. He cut downhill, not back toward the road—away from it, angling into thicker cover.

Behind him, voices sharpened.

"Stop!"

"Cut him off—left side!"

Cole didn't slow.

He vaulted a fallen trunk, landed hard, and kept moving. The ground dipped suddenly, forcing him into a slide of loose dirt and rock before he caught himself and drove forward again.

A shot cracked through the trees.

Not aimed to hit.

Close enough.

A warning.

Cole veered right, zigzagging through tighter growth. He grabbed a low branch, swung around it, and changed direction again.

He heard them closing.

Not sloppy. Not crashing blind.

They moved like they'd done this before.

Another shout. Closer now. "You're done—just stop!"

Cole ducked under a split pine and cut across a narrow game trail, boots pounding a new rhythm over packed earth. His lungs burned, but his stride held steady.

He knew this terrain better than they did.

He angled toward a shallow ravine he remembered from trail maintenance runs—steep sides, loose footing, a place that would slow anyone trying to follow fast.

The ground trembled again.

Harder.

Cole stumbled, caught himself on a tree, shoved off it, and kept going.

Behind him, one of them cursed. A body hit a bush. Another voice: “Careful—ground’s unstable—”

Good.

Cole hit the edge of the ravine and didn’t hesitate.

He jumped.

Dropped six feet, hit the slope wrong, slid on his side through dirt and loose rock before digging his boots in and forcing himself upright.

Pain flared in his shoulder.

He ignored it.

“Down there!” someone shouted.

Cole didn’t look back.

He ran along the base of the ravine, then cut sharply up the opposite side, using roots and exposed rock to pull himself up faster than they could.

A hand grabbed at his jacket from behind.

Too close.

Cole twisted hard, driving an elbow back.

It connected.

A grunt. The grip broke.

Cole surged forward, grabbing a low branch, hauling himself up the last few feet onto level ground.

He didn’t stop.

Didn’t think. He just moved.

The trees thinned slightly ahead. Too open.

He angled left again, forcing himself back into denser cover.

Another shot cracked.

Closer this time.

A bark exploded off a tree inches from his shoulder.

“Stop!” the voice snapped. Not a request anymore.

Cole dropped low, rolled behind a cluster of boulders, then came up moving again in a new direction.

They were trying to box him in.

Cut off angles and push him toward open ground.

He changed the pattern.

Slowed for two steps, then doubled back hard, slipping between two tight trees and dropping behind a fallen trunk just long enough to break the line of sight.

He stayed low.

Listened.

Boots pounded past where he’d been.

One voice: “He’s heading east—”

Another: “No, he—”

Cole moved again, silent now, controlled, putting distance between them while they chased in the wrong direction.

He climbed a small rise, crouched behind brush, and finally let himself look back.

Nothing.

No movement.

No voices.

Just wind through the trees and the distant, uneven thrum of machinery back in the clearing.

His chest heaved once, then steadied.

He wiped dirt from his face with the back of his hand and forced his breathing down.

They hadn't panicked.

They hadn't shouted threats or fired wildly.

They'd tried to contain him.

Clean. Controlled. Like procedure.

Cole straightened slowly.

Another tremor rolled through the ground—longer this time, deeper. It settled into his legs, his spine.

He looked back toward the clearing.

Toward the rigs.

Toward whatever they were pulling out of the earth.

Then he looked down at his hands.

Dirt. Blood. Not all of it is his.

They hadn't just told him to leave.

They'd tried to take him.

No warning. No questions.

Containment.

Cole's jaw tightened.

He turned and started moving again, slower now, deliberate, putting more distance between himself and the rigs.

He didn't head back toward the main roads.

Didn't head toward help.

He moved deeper into the park instead.

Because if they were willing to chase him like that—

Then he wasn't just in the way.

He was a problem.

Problems didn't get escorted out. They got erased.

CHAPTER 8

The Ground Opens

Cole hit the service road at a dead run and didn't slow down.

The trees thinned, opening onto the narrow stretch of dirt and broken asphalt that cut through the backcountry. Tire tracks from the unmarked vehicles still scarred the surface—fresh, deep, leading away from the rigs.

He followed them.

His breath came hard, steady—shoulder burning. Legs are tight but holding. He kept his pace controlled now, scanning ahead, listening behind.

Nothing is chasing him.

That didn't mean they'd stopped.

Another tremor rolled through the ground.

Longer this time.

The road shifted under his boots—just enough to feel it.

Cole slowed.

Something ahead wasn't right.

A pickup truck sat crooked across the road, engine still idling, driver's door hanging open—no one in sight.

Cole approached carefully.

"Hey!" he called out. "Anybody here?"

No answer.

The truck's front end dipped slightly toward the center of the road, as the ground beneath it had softened.

Cole stepped closer.

The air felt hotter here.

Not the normal dry heat of the basin—this was wet and heavy, pushing up from below.

Another tremor hit.

The truck creaked.

Cole stopped moving.

A low cracking sound ran under his feet.

He looked down.

A thin line split across the road.

Hairline at first.

Then it widened.

"Move," he muttered to himself, already stepping back.

The crack spread fast—snapping through the asphalt in a jagged line that shot straight toward the truck.

The ground dropped.

Not all at once.

A sudden, violent sag.

The front tires dipped into the opening as the earth beneath them collapsed.

The truck lurched forward.

Metal groaned.

The hood tipped down into the fissure as the front half of the vehicle slid into the widening gap.

Cole ran.

The ground buckled under him, splitting again, smaller fractures branching off from the main crack like lightning through dirt.

He leaped clear of one just as it tore open, heat blasting up from below.

The truck dropped further.

Half its body vanished into the earth, rear tires spinning as the engine roared.

Then the steam hit.

A burst shot up from the fissure—white, dense, scalding. It exploded outward with a deafening hiss, engulfing the truck in seconds.

Cole threw himself behind a low rise, arms over his head as the blast rolled past.

Heat slammed into him.

Wet. Burning. Suffocating.

He sucked in a breath and choked on it.

The air seared his throat.

The ground shook again.

Harder.

The rise beneath him shifted, loose dirt sliding under his chest as the tremor rolled through.

Cole pushed himself up, coughing, eyes stinging.

The road was gone.

Where the truck had been was now a jagged opening in the earth, steam pouring out in thick, relentless waves. The rear end of the vehicle jutted out at an angle, half-consumed, metal already warping under the heat.

The engine sputtered once.

Then died.

The hiss of steam filled everything.

Cole staggered back a step, boots slipping on loose gravel.

Another crack split across the edge of the road—closer this time.

He jumped back just as the ground gave way, a section collapsing into the expanding fissure with a heavy, grinding drop.

More steam surged upward.

The heat hit harder now.

Closer.

Cole turned and ran.

No path. Just distance.

The ground under him wasn't stable anymore. It shifted with every stride, small cracks snapping open and closing again like the earth couldn't decide what to do with itself.

A sharp tremor knocked him sideways.

He caught himself on a tree, bark tearing under his grip.

"Come on," he muttered, pushing off it.

Behind him, the fissure widened again with a deep, tearing sound.

Not stopping—spreading.

Cole didn't look back.

Didn't need to.

He could feel it.

The instability wasn't contained to one spot.

It was moving.

He broke through the tree line onto a narrow stretch of open ground and finally slowed, turning just enough to look over his shoulder.

Steam rose in multiple places now.

Not just the road.

The forest floor itself vented in thin, violent bursts—new cracks splitting open, closing, then opening again wider.

The fissure where the truck had fallen wasn't alone anymore. It was the same pressure—just breaking through somewhere new, wherever the ground was weakest.

It was one of many.

Cole stood there for half a second, chest heaving, heat pressing against his skin.

This wasn't contained. It wasn't slowing.

It was spreading. Not randomly following stress lines underground, moving faster each time the pressure was forced into a new location.

And fast.

CHAPTER 9

The Agent Watches

The monitors didn't match the ground.

Voss stood inside the mobile command unit, one hand braced against the edge of a console as the trailer vibrated under a passing tremor. Screens lined the walls—thermal imaging, pressure readouts, seismic graphs scrolling in tight, controlled lines.

All of it is clean.

A technician glanced over. "We're holding within projected variance."

Voss didn't look at him. "Show me basin three."

A new feed snapped onto the center screen. Heat signatures layered over terrain—color-coded, precise.

Stable.

Voss shifted his gaze to the side monitor—live drone footage from the same area.

Steam vents burst in irregular pulses. Ground discoloration spread outward in jagged patterns. Sections of terrain sagged and lifted like breath pulled too fast.

Not stable.

He reached out and tapped the screen. “Overlay.”

The technician hesitated. “It’s already—”

“Overlay the feeds.”

A pause.

Then the data is layered over the video.

For a second, it almost worked.

Then it didn’t.

The heat signatures lagged behind the actual venting. Pressure indicators stayed within range while steam columns erupted in places the system marked as inactive.

Voss leaned closer.

“Explain the delay.”

The technician swallowed. “It’s… within tolerance.”

“No,” Voss said. “It isn’t.”

Another tremor rolled through the unit, rattling equipment. A loose cable slapped against the wall.

On the far screen, a graph spiked—sharp, aggressive.

Then flattened.

Too fast.

Voss’s eyes narrowed.

“Run that again.”

“It’s already—”

"Run it again."

The technician replayed the data.

The spike appeared, then vanished, smoothed out.

Voss watched the sequence twice more, expression unchanged.

Then he reached past the technician and pulled up the raw input feed.

The spike was still there.

Higher and worse.

He switched back to the processed display.

Gone.

He didn't speak for a second.

Didn't need to.

"Who's filtering this?" he asked.

Silence.

The technician stared at the screen as if it might answer for him.

"Answer the question."

"…Central system," the technician said finally. "Automated correction."

Voss looked at him.

"Correction," he repeated.

"Yes."

Voss straightened slowly.

Another screen flickered—live drone footage shifting as the camera adjusted. A new vent tore open along a ridge line, steam blasting upward in a violent plume.

The processed data beside it barely moved.

Voss stepped back, taking in all of it at once.

Clean numbers against dirty reality.

A man in a dark jacket entered the unit, speaking as he crossed the space. “We’re maintaining containment parameters. Public narrative is stable. Media’s running the script.”

Voss didn’t turn. “The system is filtering out pressure spikes.”

The man stopped. “That’s intentional.”

“It’s inaccurate.”

“It’s controlled.”

Voss finally looked at him. “It’s wrong.”

The man’s expression didn’t change. “It’s necessary.”

Another tremor hit, stronger than the last. The floor shifted underfoot. A monitor rattled loose and swung slightly on its mount.

On the drone feed, the ridge line split further, steam venting in multiple bursts now.

The processed data has been adjusted.

Smoothed.

Contained.

Voss stepped closer to the screen.

“You’re underreporting escalation.”

“We’re managing perception.”

“You’re ignoring reality.”

The man's voice hardened. "We're preventing panic."

Voss watched the feed.

Another vent opened. Closer to the basin.

The data didn't move.

He reached out and froze the frame.

"Zoom."

The image tightened.

The ground around the new vent sagged, edges crumbling inward as heat distorted the air above it.

Voss's jaw tightened slightly.

"That's not a localized event," he said.

"No," the man replied. "It's not."

Voss looked at him.

"Then why are we treating it like one?"

"Because if we don't," the man said, "this becomes something else."

Another spike hit the raw data feed—higher than before.

The processed display flattened it instantly.

Voss watched it happen.

Watched the system erase the problem in real time. Not just smoothing noise—cutting out the spikes that showed how close the system was to failure.

His fingers hovered over the controls.

"Shut down the filters."

The technician froze. "I can't—"

"Do it."

The man stepped forward. “You don’t have that authority.”

Voss didn’t look away from the screen. “I have enough.”

“No,” the man said. “You don’t.”

A beat.

The unit hummed around them—equipment buzzing. Generators pulsing. The low, constant vibration of something building beneath the ground.

Voss’s eyes tracked the raw data again.

Another spike. Higher and closer together.

Not random. Not isolated. Stacking.

He exhaled once, slowly.

Then he stepped back from the console.

“Continue as is,” he said. Because stopping it now wouldn’t stop it—it would just take away their control.

The technician nodded quickly.

The man in the jacket relaxed—just slightly.

Voss turned toward the door.

“Where are you going?” the man asked.

“To observe,” Voss said.

“Stay within the unit.”

Voss paused at the threshold.

Then, without turning back: “Your system is lying to you.”

The man didn’t respond.

Voss stepped out into the open air.

Heat hit him immediately—thick, damp, wrong.

In the distance, another plume of steam tore upward from the tree line.

Closer than the last.

The ground under his feet shifted again.

Subtle, but there.

Voss adjusted his glasses, eyes tracking the horizon, the vents, the pattern forming, whether anyone admitted it or not.

This wasn't stabilizing. It wasn't going to settle cleanly again. The pressure had already been forced into new paths underground—places it hadn't reached before. Stopping now wouldn't undo that. It would only keep it from getting worse.

It was accelerating.

Whatever they were doing to contain it wasn't working.

CHAPTER 10

Proof

Cole circled wide before coming back.

He stayed off the road this time, cutting through timber and low brush, moving slower, quieter. The tremors came in uneven pulses now—sometimes a sharp jolt, sometimes a long roll that settled in his knees and made the trees whisper against each other.

He dropped low near the edge of the clearing.

The rigs were still running.

Louder than before.

The generators thudded in a steady, mechanical rhythm that didn't match the chaos in the ground. Steam vented in short bursts around the reinforced plates, hissing through seams that weren't meant to flex.

More men now.

More equipment.

And a perimeter.

Two guards walked a slow loop along the outer edge, heads turning just enough to check the tree line without really expecting anything to be there.

Cole watched their pattern.

Counted steps.

Timed the turn.

When one of them paused to adjust his radio, Cole moved.

He slipped from cover and crossed the open ground fast, low, using the bulk of one rig to break the line of sight. Heat rolled off the machinery, thick and damp, sticking to his skin.

He pressed himself against the metal frame and listened.

Voices nearby.

"…pressure's spiking again—"

"Then bleed it off—"

"We are. It's not enough."

Cole edged around the rig, keeping tight to the shadows, and spotted a cluster of equipment cases set beside a portable workstation—laptop open, cables running into a panel mounted at the base of the drilling collar.

No one is standing over it.

Not right now.

He moved.

Two steps.

Three.

He dropped to a knee beside the case and flipped the lid just enough to see inside—drives, tablets, printed sheets clipped in tight stacks.

He grabbed one, scanned it.

Numbers. Coordinates. Pressure readings.

Not what Voss had been looking at.

These weren't smoothed. They spiked hard.

Cole pulled his phone, snapped a quick photo, then another, angling the page to catch everything.

A shout cut across the clearing.

He froze.

Not for him.

Not yet.

"…line's unstable—check the secondary—"

Cole exhaled once, slowly, and reached for the laptop.

The screen flickered as he touched it.

Live data streamed across it—raw input, unfiltered. Graphs climbing in jagged lines, dipping, then climbing again higher.

Not contained or controlled.

He scrolled.

Another window opened—schematics.

The drilling system wasn't just tapping into the ground.

It was redirecting the flow.

Valves.

Channels.

Pressure is being pushed from one zone to another.

Cole's jaw tightened.

They weren't relieving anything. They were shifting it. Pulling pressure from one zone and forcing it into another—like plugging one leak by overloading the next. Not stopping it, redirecting it.

He snapped another photo.

Then another.

A file list caught his eye—labeled, time-stamped.

He clicked the top one.

Text filled the screen.

Operational directives. Target zones—depth markers.

One line stood out.

PRIMARY OBJECTIVE: RESOURCE EXTRACTION PRIORITY—ZONE DELTA

They weren't containing Yellowstone. They were mining it.

Cole scrolled.

Another line.

SECONDARY: PRESSURE MANAGEMENT TO MAINTAIN ACCESS

He let out a short breath through his nose.

Access to what?

He scrolled further.

A geological map appeared—layers of rock, heat zones, fault lines.

And deeper.

Highlighted in a different color.

A vein.

Marked with coordinates that didn't match any tourist map.

Not geothermal.

Not water.

Something else.

A note beside it:

HIGH-VALUE MINERAL DEPOSIT CONFIRMED

Cole stared at it.

Gold.

Another tremor hit.

The laptop rattled under his hand.

The graphs spiked again—higher than before.

Cole snapped one last photo and started to pull back.

A voice behind him said, "That's not part of the tour."

Cole didn't move.

Didn't turn.

He already knew.

He closed the laptop slowly and set it back where it had been.

Then he stood.

Turned.

The same man from before.

The one who'd seen him in the trees.

Standing ten feet away now.

No rush.

No weapon drawn.

Just watching him.

"You're persistent," the man said.

Cole didn't answer.

Another figure stepped into view off to the side.

Then another.

The perimeter had shifted.

Quietly and deliberately.

Cole's eyes flicked once—left, right, measuring distance, terrain, angles.

Fewer escape options this time.

The man smiled again, just a little.

"Let's not do the running thing again," he said.

Cole's stance shifted, weight settling into his legs.

Ready.

The ground beneath them trembled.

Harder than before.

Steam burst from one of the vents nearby, louder, more violent.

No one flinched.

The man's eyes stayed on Cole.

"Drop the phone," he said.

Cole didn't.

The tremor rolled again.

Long.

Deep.

The rigs groaned.

The man's smile faded, just slightly.

Cole saw it.

Whatever they were doing—

It was slipping.

And now they knew he knew.

Hands tightened around him.

Not touching. Yet.

He'd just crossed the line from witness—

To a problem again.

CHAPTER 11

Flip

"Drop it."

The command cut across the clearing from behind the line of men.

Cole didn't need to turn to know who it was.

The others shifted just enough to make space.

Voss stepped into view, jacket clean, glasses steady, like the ground wasn't trying to tear itself apart beneath them.

Cole held his phone in one hand, loose but not offering it.

"Perfect timing," Cole said.

Voss's eyes flicked once to the laptop, the open cases, then back to Cole. He took in the positions, the angles, the distance between bodies.

"Give me the phone," Voss said.

Cole didn't move.

"Not happening."

A man to Cole's right stepped closer. "You don't get a choice—"

"Stand down," Voss said.

The man stopped.

Cole caught that, too.

Voss stepped forward until he was within arm's reach.

Close enough that Cole could see the faint tension in his jaw now. Not fear. Not yet.

Something else.

"You've seen enough," Voss said.

"Yeah," Cole replied. "I have."

He lifted the phone slightly. "You want to tell me what this is, or you want me to start sending it out?"

Voss's gaze dropped to the device, then back to Cole's face.

"Who would you send it to?" he asked.

"Anyone who'll listen."

"No one will."

Cole gave a short laugh. "You're counting on that."

"I'm counting on time," Voss said.

The ground trembled again.

Stronger.

The rigs groaned, metal straining as the vibration rolled through them.

Cole didn't break eye contact. "You're not stabilizing anything. You're moving pressure around and hoping it doesn't blow somewhere worse."

Voss didn't answer.

Cole leaned in slightly. "You're drilling into something deeper than this system can handle."

A flicker in Voss's eyes.

Cole pushed. "You saw the data. It's not matching. You're filtering it."

"Lower your voice."

"No."

The men around them shifted again, tension tightening the space.

Cole didn't look at them.

"People are already getting hurt," he said. "You think this stays contained?"

Voss's voice stayed level. "You don't understand the scale of what—"

"Then explain it."

Steam burst from a nearby vent, louder than before.

Cole stepped closer. "You found something down there. Something worth more than the ground above it."

Voss's jaw tightened.

Cole nodded once. "Yeah. Thought so."

"Enough," Voss said.

He reached for Cole's wrist.

Cole reacted instantly, twisting, pulling back—

Hands grabbed him from both sides.

Two men locked onto his arms, forcing them down.

Cole drove a shoulder forward, trying to break the hold—

Didn't.

They were ready this time.

"Let him go," Voss said.

No one moved.

Voss's voice sharpened. "I said let him go."

The grip loosened.

Cole jerked free, stepping back into open space, chest rising and falling hard.

"You're out of your depth," Voss said quietly.

Cole barked a laugh. "You think this is about depth?"

Another tremor hit.

Violent.

The ground buckled under their feet, knocking one of the men sideways. A piece of equipment toppled, crashing against the rig.

The pipe at the base of the structure shuddered.

Hard.

A sharp crack split the air.

Everyone turned.

The valve assembly down the line jerked violently as steam forced its way through the seams. The metal casing rattled, bolts straining.

"Pressure spike!" someone shouted.

"Shut it down—!"

"We can't—"

The ground dropped.

Not far.

Not wide.

But enough.

A section of reinforced plating tilted suddenly, one side collapsing as the earth beneath it gave way.

Steam exploded upward.

Closer and hotter.

The blast knocked two men off their feet.

Cole staggered back, heat slamming into his face.

Voss didn't move fast enough.

The ground beneath him shifted, his footing slipping as the edge of the plate cracked and dropped.

Cole grabbed him.

Not a decision.

Instinct.

His hand locked onto Voss's jacket, yanking him back just as a burst of steam tore through the space where he'd been standing.

The heat roared past.

Close enough to burn.

They both hit the ground hard, rolling clear as debris rattled down around them.

Another blast.

Louder.

A second vent ruptured farther out, steam tearing through the clearing in a violent column.

Men shouted.

Equipment alarms blared.

The rigs shook.

Cole pushed himself up, dragging Voss with him. “You see it now?”

Voss coughed once, adjusting his glasses with a hand that wasn’t quite steady.

His eyes tracked the clearing.

The ruptured vent.

The collapsing plate.

The men are scrambling to regain control.

The data couldn’t be smoothed.

This wasn’t contained. It wasn’t even close.

Cole let go of him. “You keep pushing that system, it’s going to tear this place apart.”

Voss didn’t answer.

He watched another section of ground fracture, a thin line splitting outward from the main rupture.

He turned back to Cole.

Something had changed.

Not the control. Not the calculation.

But the certainty behind it.

“Give me the phone,” Voss said.

Cole held it tighter.

“No.”

Steam hissed around them. The rigs groaned under pressure. The ground vibrated in uneven pulses.

The men nearby waited.

Orders hanging in the air.

Voss looked at Cole for a long second.

Then he stepped back.

"Stand down," he said.

The men hesitated.

"Stand down."

This time, they listened.

Cole didn't move.

Didn't trust it.

Voss met his eyes. "You shouldn't be here."

"Neither should you."

Another tremor rolled through the ground.

Voss glanced toward the failing system, then back at Cole.

"You didn't see anything," he said.

Cole almost laughed. "You think I'm walking away from this?"

"I think you should."

Cole shook his head.

"Not happening."

Voss held his gaze.

Then, quietly: "Go."

The word hung there.

Cole didn't move for a second.

Then he turned.

Not running this time.

Just moving.

Fast enough to matter.

Behind him, the clearing erupted again in noise and heat.

And Voss—

Didn't stop him.

CHAPTER 12

Uneasy Alliance

Cole didn't get far before he heard footsteps behind him.

Not the chaotic rush from before—measured and controlled.

He turned.

Voss stepped out of the trees, closing the distance without urgency, like the ground wasn't shifting under both of them.

Cole didn't slow. "You've got about two seconds to explain why you're following me."

"I'm not," Voss said. "I'm redirecting."

Cole let out a dry breath. "That's a nice word for it."

Another tremor rolled underfoot.

Closer now. Stronger.

Cole angled downhill, forcing movement. Voss matched him, not as fast or as sure, but keeping pace.

"You let me walk," Cole said. "Your people don't usually make that mistake."

"They're not my people," Voss replied.

"Could've fooled me."

The ground cracked somewhere off to their left. A thin line split through the dirt, steam hissing up in a sharp burst.

Cole shifted direction instantly. "This way."

Voss hesitated half a second—just enough to show he didn't see it coming—then followed.

They cut through a stand of pines, branches snapping against Voss's jacket. He ducked late, misjudged a low limb, and caught it across the shoulder.

"You've never done this before," Cole said.

"I don't usually need to."

Another tremor hit.

The slope beneath them sagged slightly, dirt sliding under their boots. Voss stumbled, caught himself on a tree, breath tightening.

Cole didn't stop.

"Keep moving," he said.

Voss pushed off the trunk and followed.

The air felt thicker now. Hotter. Steam venting in short, violent bursts through the forest floor. The ground wasn't stable anywhere—small cracks snapping open and sealing again as pressure shifted underneath.

Cole moved faster.

"Where are we going?" Voss asked.

"Away from whatever you just broke."

“That’s not helpful.”

“It’s accurate.”

A distant roar cut across the trees.

Not wind.

Not machinery.

Something deeper.

Cole slowed just enough to listen.

Then swore under his breath. “Move.”

They broke into a run.

The trees thinned ahead, opening onto a wide stretch of low ground dotted with scrub and exposed patches of pale crust.

Bad terrain with nowhere to hide.

Cole scanned left.

Right.

Too late.

The herd hit the clearing like a wall.

Bison—dozens of them—burst through the tree line at full speed, dirt and debris exploding behind them. Their heads were low, eyes wild, bodies colliding into each other as they drove forward without any sense of direction.

“Down!” Cole barked.

Voss didn’t react fast enough.

Cole grabbed him, yanked him sideways, and shoved him behind a cluster of rocks just as the first wave tore through.

The ground shook with the impact.

Hooves hammered the earth, a deafening, chaotic thunder. One of the animals slammed into the rocks hard enough to send dust and stone flying. Another skidded, nearly going down, then surged back up and kept running.

They weren't avoiding anything.

They were running through it.

A bison veered close—too close—its shoulder clipping Voss as it passed, sending him sprawling against the rocks.

"Stay down!" Cole snapped.

Voss gritted his teeth, pushing himself up, disoriented.

"I'm fine—"

"Stay down!"

Another wave tore through the clearing, tighter, more violent. One of the animals crashed headfirst into a fallen tree, splintering it, then kept moving like it hadn't felt it.

Cole watched them.

Not panic. Not random.

"Why are they—" Voss started.

"They're running from something," Cole said.

A final surge of animals blasted past, the ground trembling under their weight.

Then they were gone.

The clearing fell into a sudden, heavy silence.

Cole rose slowly.

Voss pushed himself up beside him, breathing harder now, jacket torn at the shoulder, dirt streaked across his face.

"You said this was contained," Cole said.

Voss didn't answer.

He looked out across the clearing, tracking the direction the herd had come from.

Then he saw it.

Steam rising.

Not one plume.

Several.

In different directions.

Closer than before.

The ground trembled again.

Not sharp—rolling, building.

Cole turned. "We need to move. Now."

Voss didn't argue this time.

They ran.

The terrain shifted under them with every step. Small vents burst open, hissing violently as they passed. The air thickened, heat pressing in from all sides.

Cole took the lead without asking.

He picked the path. Adjusted on instinct, avoided ground that looked too pale, too soft, too wrong.

Voss followed. This wasn't cooperation. It was survival math.

Not graceful or fast.

But he stayed upright.

Another crack split the earth just ahead of them. Cole veered right, grabbing Voss's sleeve and dragging him with him.

"Watch your footing!"

"I am—"

"You're not."

Voss stumbled again, caught himself, and kept moving.

The ground dropped slightly behind them with a heavy, grinding sound.

Closer.

Cole didn't look back.

Didn't need to.

The instability was spreading faster than they could outrun it.

A low boom rolled across the park.

They both felt it.

Heard it.

Not close, but not far enough away.

Cole slowed just enough to turn his head.

A column of steam and debris punched up through the trees in the distance.

Then another.

And another.

Different directions, different points—all at once.

Voss stopped.

Watching.

The pattern forming.

Cole grabbed his arm. "Don't stop."

Voss didn't resist.

But his eyes stayed on the horizon.

More plumes rising.

More groundbreaking.

This wasn’t one system failing—it was all of them.

CHAPTER 13

Chain Reaction

The first blast hit behind them.

Not close—far enough to sound like a dull, rolling thud through the trees—but it carried through the ground. A low boom that traveled through the ground and up into Cole's legs like something waking up.

He didn't stop.

"Keep moving," he said, cutting left through a thinning stand of trees.

Voss followed, breathing harder now, steps uneven but holding.

Another blast.

This one sharper—steam punching through the forest canopy in a white column that rose above the treeline and spread outward like a cloud.

Then another.

Cole slowed just enough to see it.

"Not one," he muttered.

A third eruption tore upward, this time closer to the basin they'd left behind. Still behind them—but closing the distance fast. The sound cracked through the air, followed by the hiss of escaping pressure that didn't die down.

One after another.

No rhythm, no pattern that could predict.

"Chain reaction," Voss said.

He was already moving again, angling downhill toward a known trailhead—one of the faster routes back to the main road.

They broke through the last line of trees and hit the open trail.

Too many people.

Tourists clustered in loose groups, some running, some frozen, some looking back at the rising plumes, their phones still in their hands as if this were something they could record and understand later.

"Move!" Cole shouted, pushing forward. "Everyone off the trail—head west—now!"

A man grabbed his arm. "What's happening—"

"Move!" Cole shoved him in the right direction.

Another tremor hit.

Hard.

The ground buckled underfoot, a ripple that knocked several people down at once. Screams broke out, sharp and scattered.

A woman fell near the edge of the trail, her ankle twisting as she hit the dirt. She tried to stand and couldn't.

Cole was already moving toward her.

"Don't," Voss said behind him. "We don't have time—"

Cole ignored him.

He dropped beside the woman, grabbed her under the arms. "You're not walking on that. Can you put weight on it?"

"No—no-no—"

"Then you're with me."

He hauled her up, slinging her arm over his shoulder and forcing her forward.

"Stay with me," he said. "You stop, you get left behind. Understand?"

She nodded, breath shaking.

Another blast hit.

Closer.

The ground to their right split open with a sharp crack, a narrow fissure tearing across the trail. Steam vented up immediately, thick and violent.

People scattered.

Some ran straight into it.

"Back!" Cole shouted. "Back—go around—"

Too late.

A man stumbled into the edge of the fissure as it widened, his foot dropping into the gap. He screamed, scrambling back as steam blasted up around him.

Cole shoved the woman forward, passing her to another tourist. “Take her—keep moving!”

“What about—”

“Go!”

He turned back.

The fissure widened another inch, then another, the edges crumbling as the ground sagged inward.

Cole grabbed the man by the collar and yanked him free just as a fresh burst of steam erupted from below.

Heat slammed into his face.

He dragged the man back, both of them coughing as the air burned their throats.

“Move!” Cole said, shoving him toward the others.

The trail wasn’t safe anymore.

None of it was.

Another explosion hit—this one close enough to feel in his chest. A plume tore up through the trees just ahead, debris raining down across the path.

Cole looked up.

The route he’d been aiming for—

Gone.

Blocked by a fresh collapse where the ground had dropped out entirely, leaving a jagged, smoking gap where the trail used to run.

“Cole,” Voss said.

The way forward was cut off.

Behind them, more steam vents erupted in staggered bursts, sealing the path they'd come from.

Left or right.

Neither looked better.

A woman screamed from farther down the trail. "We're trapped—"

Cole stepped forward, scanning, calculating, trying to find a path that didn't end in steam or collapse.

Another tremor rolled through the ground.

Long.

Deep.

The kind that didn't stop right away.

The fissure beside them widened again, edges crumbling as the earth shifted under its own weight.

Voss stepped up beside him, breathing hard, eyes moving fast now.

"This is expanding too quickly," he said.

"No kidding."

Cole turned in a slow circle. Steam boxed them in on three sides—the only open direction was the one they'd just lost.

The terrain he knew didn't exist anymore.

Didn't exist anymore.

Steam rose in multiple columns around them, thickening the air, cutting off sightlines, turning the landscape into something unfamiliar and hostile.

Another blast hit in the distance.

Then another.

Closer.

The chain reaction wasn't slowing.

It was accelerating.

Cole looked at the people around him—scattered, panicked, waiting for direction he wasn't sure he could give.

He swallowed hard.

"Everyone listen!" he shouted. "Stay together—nobody moves without me—"

A fresh explosion cut him off.

The ground dropped somewhere just out of sight, the sound of it heavy and final.

Cole turned toward it.

Toward what should have been their way out.

Just steam.

And a widening gap in the earth where the trail had been.

They were cut off.

CHAPTER 14

Mass Casualty Event

The boardwalk shuddered.

Not a tremor.

A buckle.

Cole felt it through the soles of his boots—wood flexing, bolts groaning, something underneath giving way.

"Off the boards!" he shouted. "Now—move!"

Too slow. Too many people.

The narrow stretch ahead funneled into a raised section over a wide thermal pool, water glowing an unnatural blue beneath a skin of rising steam. Tourists packed shoulder to shoulder, trying to move, tripping over each other, nowhere to go fast enough.

The first support snapped.

A sharp crack, then another.

The boardwalk dropped six inches in the middle.

People screamed.

"Back—!" someone yelled.

Too late.

The entire section sagged, then tore free.

Wood splintered.

The center collapsed.

A mass of bodies dropped with it.

The sound—

Not just impact—water exploding.

Steam roared up in a violent burst as the structure slammed into the pool, dragging people down with it.

Cole ran. Roared

No hesitation.

He hit the edge of the break and dropped to his knees, grabbing the nearest person—a man clawing at the remaining planks, legs dangling over the edge.

"Hold on!" Cole barked.

The man slipped.

Cole caught his wrist, muscles locking as he hauled him up, dragging him back onto solid ground.

"Stay back!" Cole shoved him away. "Stay back!"

A woman flailed in the water below, her arms thrashing, skin already turning red, blistering. Another body surfaced beside her, then sank again.

The heat rolling up from the pool hit like a wall.

Cole ripped off his outer shirt, wrapped it around his hands, and dropped flat onto the edge.

"Give me your hand!" he shouted.

The woman reached.

Missed.

Reached again.

Cole lunged farther, stretching until his chest hung over the broken edge, heat searing through the fabric.

"Now!"

Their hands connected.

He grabbed her wrist and pulled.

She screamed as her legs hit the edge, skin touching the water again for a split second.

Cole gritted his teeth and hauled her up, dragging her onto the boards.

She collapsed, gasping, skin mottled and blistered.

"Don't move," he said, already turning back.

More people in the water.

Another section of the boardwalk shifted.

"Cole!"

Voss's voice cut through the chaos.

Cole looked up.

Voss stood a few feet back, frozen for half a second, eyes locked on the scene below.

Then something in him snapped into motion.

He moved forward.

Not clean or practiced.

But fast enough.

He dropped beside Cole, grabbing a loose plank and shoving it out over the water.

“Use this,” he said.

Cole didn’t argue.

They slid the plank farther out, creating a narrow extension over the pool.

“Grab it!” Cole shouted to the nearest person still fighting to stay above the surface.

A young man lunged, fingers slipping on the wet wood before catching.

“Hold!” Cole said.

Voss leaned out beside him, gripping the plank with both hands, bracing it.

His footing slipped.

Cole grabbed the back of his jacket, steadying him.

“Don’t fall in,” Cole said.

“I’m aware.”

The man in the water tried to pull himself up.

Couldn’t.

Cole shifted his grip, reached out again, grabbed the man’s arm, and hauled.

Voss leaned back, pulling with him.

Together, they dragged the man up onto the plank, then onto the boardwalk.

The man collapsed, coughing, skin already burned raw in places.

Another scream.

Cole looked back down.

A woman was slipping under.

Only her hand was visible now, clawing at the surface.

"Hold the plank," Cole said.

Voss didn't answer.

He was already moving.

He dropped flat onto the edge, farther than before, one arm extending down into the steam.

"Take it!" he shouted.

His voice cracked.

The hand caught his wrist.

For a second, it held.

Then slipped.

Voss lunged farther, his body nearly over the edge now.

Cole grabbed his belt, anchoring him.

"Don't—"

"I've got her—"

The ground shifted.

Hard.

The remaining structure lurched.

Wood snapped somewhere behind them.

"Pull!" Cole shouted.

Voss strained, face tightening, glasses slipping down his nose.

The woman's hand locked onto his again.

This time, it held.

Cole pulled them both back.

Together, they dragged her onto the boards just as another section of the walkway gave way with a splintering crack.

More debris dropped into the pool.

Steam exploded upward again.

Cole shoved both survivors back. “Away from the edge!”

He pushed himself up, scanning.

The collapse had widened.

What had been a narrow crossing was now a jagged gap, the thermal pool exposed, boiling, swallowing everything that fell into it.

People stumbled away, crying, screaming, some in shock, some burned, some just staring.

Voss stood beside him, breathing hard, hands shaking slightly.

He didn’t hide it.

Didn’t try.

Cole glanced at him once.

Then looked away.

“Everyone off this structure!” Cole shouted. “Move back—now!”

People moved.

Faster this time.

Fear had finally caught up.

A voice crackled over a nearby radio.

“…all exits compromised—repeat, all exits compromised—roads are—”

Static swallowed the rest.

Another voice cut in, sharper. “South access is gone—bridge collapse—”

Cole grabbed the radio from a fallen ranger nearby and keyed it.

“Say again—what’s gone?”

Static.

Then: “North exit blocked—ground failure—no vehicles getting through—”

Cole’s grip tightened on the radio.

“East?”

“Steam vents across the road—can’t pass—”

The line cut out.

Cole lowered the radio slowly.

Around him, the park wasn’t just unstable.

It was closing.

Routes gone.

Access points are collapsing.

Containment—real or not—didn’t matter anymore.

There was nowhere left to go.

Voss stood beside him, staring out over the ruined boardwalk, the boiling pool, the rising steam.

Then he looked up.

Toward the tree line.

Toward the direction the rest of the park stretched.

More plumes rising.

Closer.

Cole followed his gaze.

And felt it settle.

Not panic. Not yet.

They weren't evacuating anyone.

Not anymore.

They were trapped inside it.

CHAPTER 15

No Exit

They moved fast and got nowhere.

Cole pushed the group along a service road that should have cut straight to the west access. It didn't.

The asphalt ahead was broken in three places, each split running across the road like a jagged seam. Heat shimmered up from the cracks. Thin lines of steam bled out, hissing like something breathing under the surface.

"Stay off the edges," Cole said. "Single file. Watch your footing."

People nodded. Didn't slow.

They were past questions.

A tremor rolled through the ground.

The nearest fissure widened an inch with a dry, tearing sound.

"Move," Cole snapped.

He jumped the gap, landed hard, turned, and reached back. One by one, he hauled people across—hands grabbing wrists, shoes scraping, a man slipping and catching himself at the last second.

Voss crossed last.

He didn't jump clean. Hit the far side awkwardly, stumbled, and nearly went down.

Cole caught his arm and pulled him upright. "Stay on your feet."

"I'm trying."

"Try faster."

They pushed on.

The road dipped and curved. A park truck sat sideways up ahead, nose buried into a fresh collapse where the ground had dropped out entirely. The rear wheels spun slowly, useless, engine whining like it didn't understand it had nowhere left to go.

Cole stopped.

Looked, measured.

The collapse ran deep—ten feet across, maybe more. Steam rolled up from the bottom in thick waves. The edges crumbled even as he watched.

"Back," he said. "We find another route."

A man shook his head, voice breaking. "There is no other route."

Cole didn't argue.

He turned them off the road and into the brush.

Ash drifted down through the trees.

Light at first—fine gray flakes settling on shoulders, catching in hair, sticking to damp skin.

Cole looked up.

The sky had changed.

Not dark. Not yet.

But hazed over, the blue fading behind a thin veil that hadn't been there an hour ago.

"Keep moving," he said.

They moved.

Branches snapped. Shoes slid on loose dirt. Someone coughed—once, then again, harsher.

Voss pulled his jacket up over his mouth, eyes scanning the horizon through the thinning trees.

"Wind's carrying it," he said.

"Yeah."

"From where?"

Cole didn't answer.

Another tremor hit.

Long.

Heavy.

The kind that didn't feel like it ended so much as faded.

A line of trees ahead shifted—just slightly—then one tilted, roots lifting as the ground beneath it sagged.

It went over with a cracking snap.

People flinched. One woman cried out.

Cole cut right, forcing them around it. "Stay together—don't spread out!"

A radio crackled somewhere behind them.

"...all units—repeat—all units—perimeter lockdown in effect—"

Static.

"Rescue operations are suspended until further—"

Cole grabbed the radio from the ranger. "Say that again—who's suspended?"

Static.

"...containment priority—"

"Containment?" Cole snapped. "There are civilians out here—"

The signal died.

Gone.

He lowered the radio slowly.

Around him, people were watching his face.

Waiting.

"What did they say?" someone asked.

Cole didn't answer.

He handed the radio back.

"Keep moving."

A man stepped into his path. "No—tell us what they said."

Cole met his eyes.

"They're not coming," he said.

The words landed.

The man stepped back.

No argument left.

They moved again.

Faster now.

Not because there was a plan—because stopping felt worse.

The ground shifted under them again, a series of quick, uneven jolts. Small cracks snapped open at their feet, then sealed again, like the surface couldn't decide what it wanted to do.

Steam vented through the forest floor in sharp bursts.

Closer.

More frequent.

Voss stumbled again, caught himself against a tree, breath tight.

Cole slowed just enough to keep him upright. "You good?"

"Define good."

"Can you move?"

"Yes."

"Then move."

They pushed through a final line of trees and broke into another open stretch.

A road lay ahead.

Or what had been one.

It was gone.

Not blocked—gone.

The entire section had collapsed into a wide, smoking trench that stretched as far as they could see in either direction. Steam poured up from it in thick, rolling clouds. The far side was visible through the haze—but unreachable.

Cole stepped to the edge.

Looked down.

Nothing but heat, depth, and the sound of something shifting below.

He stepped back.

Behind them, the trees hissed with new vents opening.

Above them, ash fell thicker now.

Not enough to choke.

Enough to notice.

Voss came up beside him.

"This was the west access?"

"Yeah."

"It's not anymore."

Cole nodded once.

He turned, scanning behind them.

Steam rising.

Ground shifting.

Paths closing.

A woman's voice broke, quiet this time. "Where do we go?"

Cole didn't answer right away.

He didn't have one.

For the first time since this started, there wasn't a direction he trusted.

Another tremor rolled through.

Deeper.

Closer.

The trench in front of them shifted, edges crumbling inward with a slow, grinding drop.

Cole looked at it.

Then, the people behind him.

Then back at the park.

And understood it.

Not in pieces, not as a series of bad events.

As a whole.

This wasn't something they could outrun.

Not anymore.

They weren't trying to get out of Yellowstone.

They were inside it.

And it was closing around them.

CHAPTER 16

Acceleration

The ground didn't settle anymore.

Cole felt it in every step—small, constant vibrations stacking on top of each other until walking felt like trying to move across something alive.

"Keep your spacing," he said. "If it drops, you don't all go with it."

People nodded. Some listened, some didn't.

The ash came down thicker now, drifting sideways through the trees, catching in throats, turning breaths shallow and sharp.

A woman coughed behind him, then again, harder.

"Cover your mouth," Cole said. "Shirts, sleeves—anything."

There was no direction anymore that felt right.

Another tremor rolled through.

The ground shuddered in a continuous, uneven pulse.

"Is it supposed to do this?" someone asked.

"No," Cole said.

Ahead, the forest floor lifted slightly, then dropped back down with a soft, unsettling thud. Steam pushed up through the seams, thicker than before, turning the air damp and heavy.

Cole veered right, avoiding a pale stretch of ground that looked too smooth, too soft.

Voss followed, slower now, his steps less certain with each shift underfoot.

"You're adjusting direction without a map," he said.

"Map's wrong now."

"That's not reassuring."

Cole didn't answer.

Another crack split the earth ahead of them, a thin line that widened just enough to hiss steam into the air before sealing again.

Temporary. Nothing stayed open or closed.

Voss stopped for a second, scanning the terrain, eyes tracking the pattern—the vents, the cracks, the way they were clustering closer together.

"This isn't isolated," he said.

"It's not even regional."

Cole glanced at him. "You just figured that out?"

Voss ignored the edge in his voice. "The pressure redistribution isn't stabilizing anything. It's cascading."

Cole slowed just enough to face him. "Say that in English."

Voss gestured toward the ground. "You move pressure from one point; it builds somewhere else. They're chasing it instead of controlling it."

"They're making it worse."

Another tremor hit.

Hard enough to knock a man off balance behind them.

Cole grabbed him, shoved him upright. "Stay on your feet."

The man nodded, wide-eyed, shaking.

Cole turned back to Voss. "Then shut it down."

Voss didn't answer.

Cole stepped closer. "You hear me? Whatever they're doing—stop it."

Voss looked past him, toward the direction of the rigs, eyes narrowing.

"It's not that simple."

"Yeah, it is."

"No," Voss said. "It isn't."

Another pulse rolled through the ground, deeper this time, longer, like something gathering itself.

Voss spoke over it. "If they cut the system now—"

"Then it stops."

"No," Voss said. "Then it releases."

Cole stared at him.

"All of it," Voss continued. "At once. No redistribution. No delay."

Cole's jaw tightened. "So what—you just keep pushing it around until it blows somewhere else?"

Voss didn't respond.

A distant rumble rolled across the park.

Lower than the explosions before.

Heavier.

Cole turned toward it.

A column of steam rose in the distance, wider than anything they'd seen yet, spreading at the top like a slow, blooming cloud.

Another followed.

Closer.

The ground under them didn't just tremble now.

It surged.

A wave moving through the earth.

People stumbled. One fell. Another screamed.

Cole grabbed the nearest shoulder and hauled the person back up. "Move!"

They moved.

Because stopping wasn't an option anymore.

Voss pulled something from his jacket—a compact device, screen flickering to life.

He stared at it.

Numbers scrolled.

Not smoothed.

Not filtered.

Raw.

His expression tightened.

Cole saw it. "What is it?"

Voss didn't answer right away.

His thumb moved across the screen, pulling up another feed.

Another set of numbers.

Higher.

Closer together.

"No," he said, almost to himself.

Cole stepped closer. "What?"

Voss looked up.

"This isn't linear."

"Meaning?"

"It's accelerating faster than the system can compensate."

Cole gave a short, sharp breath. "Yeah. I got that part."

Voss shook his head once. "No, you don't. It's not just failing. It's feeding itself now."

Another tremor hit.

Stronger.

The ground ahead dropped several inches, then held.

Cole looked at him. "Then shut it down."

Voss's gaze flicked back to the device.

Then toward the horizon.

Then back again.

"They won't."

"Then make them."

Voss didn't move.

Didn't speak.

The device in his hand crackled.

A voice came through—tight, controlled.

"…initiating final sequence—"

Voss froze.

Cole saw it. "What is that?"

Voss lifted the device slightly, listening.

"…pressure thresholds exceeded—proceeding with full release protocol—"

Cole grabbed his arm. "What does that mean?"

Voss looked at him.

For the first time—not controlled, not detached.

"Everything," he said.

Another rumble rolled through the ground.

Deeper than anything before.

The air itself seemed to tighten.

Cole's grip tightened on his arm. "Stop it."

Voss didn't move.

Didn't answer.

The voice on the device continued, calm, precise.

"…final procedure engaged…"

CHAPTER 17

The Sky Changes

The ash didn't drift anymore.

It fell.

Thicker, heavier—turning the air gray in slow layers that swallowed the light one piece at a time.

Cole pulled his shirt up over his mouth and kept moving.

"Keep your faces covered!" he shouted. "Don't breathe it in!"

People tried.

Some coughed anyway.

A man bent double behind him, hacking, shoulders shaking. The sound scraped raw, like he couldn't get air deep enough to matter.

"Stay with us," Cole said, grabbing his arm and hauling him forward. "Don't stop."

The man nodded, eyes watering, and stumbled on.

The sky dimmed.

Not like clouds.

Like something was taking the light away.

The sun blurred behind the ash, reduced to a pale smear that gave off more glow than heat. Shadows flattened. Colors drained out of everything—trees, dirt, faces—all of it fading toward the same dull gray.

Another tremor rolled through.

Constant now.

Not spikes, not bursts.

Just a steady, uneven motion under their feet that never quite stopped.

Voss walked beside Cole, slower, breathing harder, one hand still pressed to his face.

"This is increasing faster than projected," he said, voice muffled.

"Yeah," Cole replied. "I noticed."

Voss glanced up.

Then stopped.

Cole grabbed his sleeve. "Don't—"

"Listen."

Cole didn't want to.

He did anyway.

No birds.

No wind in the branches.

No distant movement.

Just the hiss of steam and the low, constant vibration under the ground.

The park had gone quiet.

Not calm—empty.

Cole scanned the tree line.

Nothing moved.

No animals breaking through.

No sound of anything alive beyond the people with him.

"They're gone," someone whispered.

Cole didn't answer.

He didn't need to.

Another tremor.

The ground shifted enough to throw a few people off balance. A woman fell to her knees, palms hitting the dirt hard.

Cole hauled her up. "Stay on your feet."

"I can't—"

"You can."

He pushed her forward.

The air thickened again.

Breathing got harder.

Each inhale felt shallow, incomplete, as if the ash were filling the space before oxygen could.

People slowed.

Cole didn't let them.

"Keep moving!" he shouted. "Don't stop!"

A man stumbled, coughed hard, then harder, dropping to one knee.

Voss moved without thinking, grabbing him under the arm, hauling him back up like he was already calculating whether helping would cost him more than standing still.

"Move," he said, sharper now. "You stop, you're done."

The man nodded, eyes wide, and forced himself forward.

Cole glanced at Voss.

Different—less controlled, more present.

Another rumble rolled through the ground.

Not a tremor—deeper, sustained.

Cole stopped.

This time, he couldn't help it.

The sound built under them, low and heavy, like something shifting at a scale too large to see.

Voss looked up.

So did everyone else.

The horizon had changed.

The distant tree line blurred behind a rising wall of gray and white—steam, ash, something else pushing upward in a slow, expanding column.

Bigger than the others—much bigger.

Cole felt it in his chest.

"Move," he said, quieter now. "We need to move."

No one argued.

They moved.

As fast as they could, with the ground shifting and the air choking them.

The rumble didn't stop.

It grew.

Another crack split the earth ahead, wider than the others, steam blasting up in a violent burst that forced them to veer hard around it.

Cole grabbed Voss's sleeve, pulling him clear.

"Watch it!"

"I am—"

"You're not."

Voss didn't respond.

His eyes were on the horizon.

On the rising column.

It spread at the top now, darkening the sky around it, pushing the ash cloud outward in a widening circle.

Cole saw it too.

Felt it.

Whatever had been building—

It wasn't far anymore.

And it wasn't small.

A woman behind them sobbed, voice breaking. "What is that?"

Cole didn't answer.

He couldn't.

Because he already knew.

This wasn't another vent, not another fissure, not something they could move around.

This was bigger.

Closer.

And it was coming.

CHAPTER 18

Final Mistake

The ground dropped under Cole's left foot.

Not a crack. Not a tremor.

A sudden, hollow give that made him yank his leg back just as the soil collapsed into a narrow opening, steam blasting up hard enough to sting his face through the cloth.

"Keep moving!" he shouted, dragging the line of people past it. "Don't bunch up!"

They pushed forward in a staggered line, coughing, stumbling, eyes locked on him because he was the only thing that felt like direction.

Voss slowed.

Not from exhaustion.

From listening.

Cole grabbed his sleeve. "Not now."

Voss pulled free, turning slightly, his head angled as if trying to separate one sound from all the others.

"Wait."

"No," Cole said. "We don't wait."

"Listen."

Cole didn't want to.

He did anyway.

Under the constant rumble—under the tremors, the hiss of steam, the coughing and shouting—there was something else.

A pattern.

Low. Rhythmic.

Mechanical.

Voss looked down at the device in his hand. The screen flickered, numbers jumping in tight clusters, then spiking hard.

"They've started it," he said.

Cole stared at him. "Started what?"

Voss didn't answer.

The sound changed.

Not louder—sharper.

Like pressure being forced through something too small to hold.

Cole turned toward the rigs.

Through the trees, a column of steam punched up—straight, violent, controlled for half a second—

Then it widened.

Exploded outward.

The ground jumped under their feet.

A second column followed.

Then a third.

Not random—timed.

Cole felt it hit him.

"They're venting it," he said.

Voss shook his head. "No."

Another surge of pressure ripped through the earth. A line of trees ahead snapped sideways as the ground beneath them shifted.

"What do you mean, no?" Cole snapped.

"They're not venting," Voss said. "They're forcing it."

A deep crack split the air.

Closer.

The ground in front of them tore open in a jagged line, wider than any fissure before. Steam blasted out in a thick, violent column, forcing them to veer hard around it.

People screamed.

Cole shoved them through, keeping them moving, forcing momentum back into bodies that wanted to freeze.

Behind them, another eruption punched upward.

Then another.

The pattern broke. The system didn't hold—it scattered.

Columns rose in different directions now, not controlled, not contained—just pressure ripping through wherever it could find space.

Voss looked at the device again.

The numbers climbed.

Higher, faster.

"They pushed too hard," he said.

Cole grabbed his arm. "Fix it."

"It's past that."

"Then shut it down."

Voss didn't respond.

Another tremor hit.

This one didn't roll—it slammed.

The ground bucked hard enough to knock several people off their feet. Cole caught one, shoved another upright, dragging them forward as the terrain shifted under them.

"Move!" he shouted. "Move!"

A roar built in the distance.

Not steam.

Not steam, not the sharp crack of a vent—something deeper.

Cole turned his head.

Through the ash and steam, the horizon shifted again.

A column rose.

Wider than before, darker at the base.

It didn't stop.

Didn't taper.

It kept climbing, pushing through the cloud layer, spreading outward at the top like something breaking through a barrier.

Voss saw it too.

His voice dropped. "No."

Cole didn't ask.

He already knew.

Another eruption hit closer.

The ground split again, wider this time, the edges collapsing inward as heat blasted up from below.

People scattered, breaking formation.

Cole chased them down, grabbing their shoulders and pulling them back into a line.

"Stay together!" he shouted. "You split, you're done!"

Another column rose behind them.

Then another.

Multiple points.

All at once.

No control, no pattern left.

Voss looked down at the device one last time.

The screen glitched.

Numbers spiked.

Then vanished.

He lowered it slowly.

"They triggered a full release," he said.

Cole stared at him. "You said that would—"

"I know what I said."

Another roar cut him off.

Closer.

The air itself seemed to tighten.

The ground didn't just tremble now—it surged.

A deep, sustained movement that didn't stop.

Didn't fade.

Cole felt it in his chest, his teeth, his bones.

The column on the horizon expanded again.

Faster now.

The base darkened.

Thickened.

Cole grabbed the nearest person and shoved them forward.

"Run!"

No more direction.

No more path.

Just distance.

The roar built.

Not behind them, not ahead—everywhere.

Cole didn't look back again.

Didn't need to.

Because whatever they'd triggered—

It wasn't stopping. It was moving.

It was starting.

CHAPTER 19

The Eruption

The sound hit before the blast.

A deep, tearing roar that didn't belong to anything human—too wide, too heavy—ripping through the ground and the air at the same time.

Cole felt it in his chest.

Then the world punched back.

The shockwave slammed into them like a wall. It knocked people flat, drove the air out of Cole's lungs, sent him skidding across dirt and ash as trees snapped and branches tore loose overhead.

"Down!" he tried to shout, but it came out broken.

The ground surged again. From behind—pushing everything forward, whether they were ready or not.

Not a tremor—a heave.

Cole clawed at the dirt, forcing himself upright as debris rained down around him—ash, rock, splintered wood.

The sky tore open.

A massive column of ash and steam punched upward, wider than anything before, black at the base, churning as it climbed. It didn't stop. It spread outward, blotting out what little light remained.

People screamed.

Some didn't get back up.

Cole staggered to his feet, grabbing the nearest arm and hauling a man upright. "Move!"

The man stumbled, disoriented, eyes wide and empty.

Another shockwave rolled through.

Weaker.

But close enough to knock them sideways again.

Cole shoved the man forward. "Run!"

The air changed.

Hotter, drier.

Then suddenly—

Burning.

Cole turned.

Through the trees, a wall moved.

Not flame—not exactly.

A dense, fast-moving surge of heat and ash tears through the forest, flattening everything in its path. Trees snapped as it hit them, trunks splintering, branches igniting or blasting apart under the force.

"Go!" Cole shouted. "Now—run!"

He grabbed Voss's sleeve and dragged him forward.

Voss stumbled, caught himself, then ran.

Not well, not clean.

But fast enough.

The surge behind them gained ground.

Cole could hear it—like a freight train ripping through timber, tearing the world apart behind them.

"Left!" Cole shouted, veering hard.

They cut downhill.

Bad footing.

Loose soil.

Cole slid, caught himself, and kept moving. People followed, some falling, some scrambling back up, all of them driven by the same thing—

The sound behind them.

Closer. Too close.

Heat hit their backs.

Not direct—but enough.

Cole felt it through his shirt, through his skin.

"Don't stop!" he yelled. "Don't look back!"

A man did.

He slowed.

Half a second.

That was all it took.

The surge hit him.

Not fully—just the edge.

It knocked him forward, rolled him, and when he came up again, his skin was already reddening, clothes smoking.

He screamed.

Cole didn't stop.

Couldn't.

He grabbed the next person and shoved them forward. "Keep moving!"

The ground cracked open ahead.

A wide fissure tore across their path, steam blasting up in a violent column.

Cole skidded to a stop, grabbed the nearest two people, and yanked them sideways just as the ground dropped further.

"Go around!" he shouted.

They split, scrambling along the edge, slipping on loose ash, coughing as the air thickened again.

The sky above them went darker.

Not dim—dark.

The ash column spread outward, turning daylight into something that barely reached the ground.

Cole's chest burned.

Each breath came shorter, shallower.

He forced himself forward.

One step.

Then another.

Voss stumbled beside him, nearly going down.

Cole grabbed him, hauled him upright. "Stay up!"

"I—" Voss coughed hard, choking on the air. "I can't—"

"You can."

Cole dragged him another few feet, then shoved him forward. "Move!"

Another blast hit.

Closer.

A section of forest ahead exploded outward as a vent tore open beneath it, trees lifting, then collapsing as steam and debris ripped through them.

Cole changed direction again.

No plan—just reaction.

The ground wasn't stable anywhere.

The air wasn't breathable.

The sky wasn't visible.

And the thing behind them—

Wasn't slowing.

Cole felt it.

The heat is building.

The pressure.

The sense of something massive closing in.

He pushed harder.

Faster.

But it didn't matter.

The surge gained.

The world narrowed to movement and sound and heat.

A woman fell.

Cole grabbed her, pulled her up, and shoved her forward.

“Don’t stop!”

She ran.

Barely.

But she ran.

Another shockwave rippled through the ground, knocking several people down at once.

Cole hit hard, rolled, came up on one knee, dragging himself upright again.

His legs burned.

His lungs burned.

Everything burned.

He looked ahead.

No clear path, no safe ground.

Just more collapsing terrain, more steam, more ash choking the air.

He looked back.

The surge filled the space between the trees now, closer than ever, tearing through everything in its way.

There was no outrunning it.

No outmaneuvering it, no getting ahead of it.

Cole turned forward again, grabbing Voss and the nearest person, forcing them into motion one more time.

But the truth hit him hard and clean.

They weren't escaping this.

They were inside it.

And it was closing fast.

CHAPTER 20

Survival Run

"Follow me!"

Cole didn't slow as he cut hard downhill, forcing the group into a narrow line through a break in the trees. The ground shifted under every step—loose, sliding, unreliable—but downhill meant distance, and distance was the only thing left.

"Stay close!" he shouted. "Don't spread out!"

The surge behind them roared louder.

The air burned hotter now, ash thick enough to taste with every breath. People coughed, stumbled, and kept moving because stopping wasn't an option anymore.

Cole angled left, avoiding a pale stretch of ground that sagged under its own weight. Still driving downhill, away from the basin—but into terrain he no longer recognized. He jumped a narrow crack, turned, grabbed the next person, and hauled them across.

“Go!”

They moved as fast as they could.

The terrain dropped again—steeper this time, a slope of loose dirt and rock sliding under their feet.

“Slide it!” Cole shouted. “Stay low—don’t fight it!”

He dropped first, boots digging in, controlling the descent as best he could. Dirt and ash cascaded around him, stinging his eyes, coating his throat.

He hit the bottom hard, rolled, and came up fast.

“Move!”

People slid down after him—some controlled, some not. A man lost his footing halfway and tumbled, hitting the bottom hard and not getting up right away.

Cole grabbed him, yanked him upright. “You’re good—move!”

“I—”

“Move!”

The man moved.

Voss came down last.

He slipped early, hit the slope wrong, and slid hard, picking up speed as loose ground gave way under him.

“Voss!” Cole shouted.

Voss tried to stop.

Couldn’t.

He slammed into the bottom, shoulder first, momentum carrying him straight toward a new crack splitting open at the base of the slope.

The fissure widened as he slid.

Steam blasted up.

Cole ran.

He hit the edge just as Voss's body slid into it.

Cole dove, grabbing his jacket, locking his grip just as the ground beneath Voss dropped another inch.

Heat surged up from below.

Voss twisted, trying to get footing, but there was none—just loose dirt crumbling away under him.

"Hold still!" Cole snapped.

"I'm trying—"

"Don't move!"

Cole planted his boots, leaned back, and hauled.

The ground shifted again.

The edge gave slightly under Cole's weight.

He tightened his grip and pulled harder.

Voss's hand found the edge, fingers digging into dirt that didn't want to hold.

Another tremor hit.

Hard.

The fissure widened again.

Cole gritted his teeth and yanked.

Voss came free in a sudden jerk, both of them falling backward onto solid ground as steam exploded upward where he'd been.

Breathing hard.

Then Cole grabbed him and dragged him upright. "We're not done—move!"

Voss didn't argue.

Didn't hesitate.

They ran.

The ground ahead shifted again—small collapses, vents bursting open, the air thick with heat and ash.

Cole cut right, then left, picking a path on instinct alone now.

"Stay with me!" he shouted back. "Don't lose me!"

A roar built behind them.

Closer.

The surge is tearing through the forest, flattening everything in its path.

Cole pushed harder.

Faster.

He spotted it ahead.

A break in the terrain.

Not a road—not exactly.

But a strip of ground that looked more stable than anything else—less cracked, less venting.

"Through there!" he shouted.

They ran for it.

The ground buckled under their feet as they closed the distance. A crack snapped open just behind them, swallowing a section of earth with a heavy, final drop.

No going back.

Cole didn't look.

Didn't need to.

They hit the strip of ground at full speed.

For a second—

It held.

Cole didn't slow.

"Keep going!"

The air thinned slightly here.

Still ash-filled, still burning.

They pushed forward, bodies moving on momentum alone now.

Voss stumbled again.

Cole caught him without breaking stride, dragging him upright. "Stay with me!"

"I'm—" Voss coughed hard. "I'm trying—"

"Try harder!"

The edge of the strip came into view.

Beyond it—

Open ground.

Wider.

Clearer.

A possible way out.

Cole felt it.

The first real chance they'd had.

People surged forward, desperation turning into something sharper.

Hope.

They hit the edge.

The ground ahead was gone.

Not collapsed—cut.

A wide, smoking trench stretched across their path, deeper and broader than anything they'd seen before. Steam poured out in thick, violent waves, the far side visible through the haze—

Close enough to see, too far to reach.

Cole stepped to the edge.

Looked down.

Nothing but heat and depth and the sound of something shifting far below.

Behind them, the roar grew louder.

Closer.

No time, no space, no path forward.

Cole turned back to the group, then to Voss.

One last obstacle.

CHAPTER 21

The Cost

The trench roared.

Heat rolled up in waves, thick and wet, carrying the smell of scorched earth and something worse. The far side sat there—so close it hurt to look at, a strip of ground that might hold if they could reach it.

Behind them, the surge closed.

Louder, closer

Cole turned. "We're going across."

A man stared at him. "That's not a jump."

"It is today."

Cole scanned fast.

A fallen tree lay half-burned along the edge, trunk splintered but intact enough to move.

"Help me!" he snapped.

Two people stepped forward.

Three.

They grabbed the trunk, dragging it toward the edge, boots slipping on ash, hands burning where bark had heated under the air.

“Push!” Cole barked.

They shoved together.

The tree slid, then tipped, one end dropping into the trench with a heavy crack.

Steam exploded up around it.

The trunk bounced once.

Settled.

Barely spanning the gap—one end resting on their side, the other catching on the far edge, unstable, angled, slick with ash.

Cole didn’t wait.

“I go first.”

He stepped onto it.

The wood shifted under his weight, groaning.

He moved fast, low, balancing, ignoring the heat rising through the soles of his boots.

Halfway across—

The trunk shifted.

Slipped.

Cole dropped to a knee, grabbed for balance, heart slamming.

The far end held.

Barely.

He pushed up and lunged the last step, hitting the other side hard and turning immediately.

"Come on!" he shouted. "One at a time—fast!"

The first person ran.

The trunk rocked, nearly throwing them off, but they made it, collapsing onto the far side.

"Next!"

They came.

One by one.

Some steady.

Some not.

Cole grabbed wrists, hauled people over, shoved them clear.

Behind them, the roar built.

The surge pushed closer, heat licking at their backs.

"Move!" Cole shouted. "Move!"

A woman froze halfway across, knees shaking, unable to take the next step.

"I can't—"

"Yes, you can!" Cole yelled. "Look at me—don't look down—come on!"

She shook her head.

The trunk shifted again.

Cole stepped back onto it.

Voss grabbed his arm. "Don't—"

Cole pulled free. "I've got her."

He moved out, careful, controlled, reaching her.

“Give me your hand.”

She hesitated.

Another blast of heat rolled up from below.

“Now!” Cole snapped.

She grabbed him.

He pulled her forward, guiding her step by step until she stumbled onto solid ground.

“Go!” he said, pushing her away.

He turned back.

More people are waiting.

Fewer now.

A man stepped onto the trunk—

And slipped.

His foot slid off the side, body twisting as he tried to recover.

He didn’t.

He dropped.

The scream cut off as steam swallowed him.

The trunk jolted hard.

People cried out.

Cole froze for half a second.

Then forced himself to move.

“Next!” he shouted.

No one moved.

“Next!” louder now.

Voss stepped forward.

“I’ll go.”

Cole nodded once.

Voss moved onto the trunk, slower, more careful, arms out for balance. He nearly slipped twice, catching himself at the last second, but he made it across, collapsing onto the far side beside Cole.

Cole grabbed his jacket and hauled him upright. "You're not done."

Voss nodded, breathing hard.

Another person ran across.

Then another.

Each one is riskier.

Each step is less stable.

The trunk shifted more with every crossing.

Behind them, the surge broke through the tree line.

Cole saw it.

Felt it.

"Last two!" he shouted.

A man and a woman moved together.

"Separate!" Cole snapped.

They stepped onto the trunk at the same time.

It dipped.

Shifted.

The far end slipped.

The woman screamed.

Cole lunged forward, grabbing her arm as she slid, pulling her toward him.

The man lost his footing completely.

He went over.

No time to react, no way to reach him.

Cole dragged the woman up onto solid ground, pushing her back.

"Go!"

She ran.

Didn't look back.

Cole turned.

The trunk shifted again.

The far end slipped further.

Not going to hold.

The surge roared closer.

Cole stepped off the trunk just as it dropped, the far end sliding into the trench and disappearing into the steam below.

Gone.

No way back.

He stood there for half a second, chest heaving, heat pressing in from behind.

Then he turned.

"Move!" he shouted.

They ran.

But moving.

Always moving.

Voss fell into step beside him, still breathing hard, still upright.

Cole pulled his phone from his pocket mid-stride, checking it.

Cracked screen.

Still on.

The photos—

Still there.

Proof.

He shoved it back into his pocket and pushed forward.

The ground ahead looked clearer.

Less broken.

Less venting.

But survivable.

Behind them, the surge hit the trench.

Steam exploded upward.

The roar swallowed everything.

Cole didn't look back again.

Didn't stop.

Because stopping meant ending.

And they weren't there yet.

They broke through the last line of trees into open ground—

And for the first time since it started—

There was space.

Cole slowed.

Just a fraction.

Breathing hard.

Body shaking.

Alive.

Barely.

But alive.

He looked at Voss.

Then, the survivors around them.

Then back at the park behind them.

Burning.

Breaking.

Still moving.

They'd made it out.

But only just.

CHAPTER 22

Dark Ending

The sky never cleared.

Not that day, not the next.

Ash hung over everything, turning daylight into a dull, colorless glow that never quite broke through. What had been forest was now stripped, blackened, flattened in wide arcs that followed no clean pattern—just damage layered on damage, as far as the eye could carry.

Yellowstone still stood.

But it wasn't the same place—not even close.

Cole stood at the edge of a secured perimeter, days later, boots planted in dirt that no longer felt like ground. It felt hollow now, warped.

Helicopters moved overhead in steady rotations. Trucks came and went. Barriers stretched farther out than before, pushing people back from what was left of the park.

He watched a line of officials step out near the mobile units, their voices low, controlled, their movements deliberate. Cameras waited at a distance, lenses angled carefully, capturing only what they were allowed to see.

"Localized geothermal event."

"Unexpected pressure release."

"Limited impact."

Cole exhaled once through his nose.

Behind the perimeter, the land told a different story.

Collapsed sections where trails used to run.

Blackened zones where heat had rolled through too fast to outrun.

Pools that had shifted, expanded, or vanished entirely.

The system hadn't stabilized.

It had settled.

Footsteps approached.

Cole didn't turn.

"You're not supposed to be here," Voss said.

Cole let that sit.

"Neither are you."

Voss stopped beside him.

No suit now, no clean lines.

Just the same jacket, worn at the shoulder where it had torn, ash still worked into the seams, no matter how many times it had been brushed off.

He looked out over the damage.

Didn't speak right away.

"They've rewritten the reports," Voss said finally.

Cole nodded. "Figured."

"Data's been adjusted. Timelines compressed. Causation… simplified."

"Yes."

Cole shifted his weight, eyes still on the horizon.

"You going to sign off on it?"

Voss didn't answer immediately.

A helicopter passed overhead, the sound heavy, mechanical, indifferent.

"I already have," he said.

Cole let out a short breath.

"Of course you did."

Voss didn't react to it.

"They're calling it contained," he added.

Cole looked at him then.

"Is it?"

Voss held his gaze.

"No," he said.

Cole looked back at the park.

Steam still rose in thin, irregular lines across the landscape. Not violent anymore. Not explosive.

But not right either.

The ground still shifted sometimes—small, subtle movements that most people wouldn't notice.

Cole did.

He always would now.

A truck passed behind them, carrying equipment away from the inner perimeter, not shutting it down.

Relocating it.

Cole caught that.

"Going back in?" he asked.

Voss followed his line of sight.

"Eventually."

"To do what?"

"Continue."

Cole almost laughed.

Didn't.

"They didn't learn anything," he said.

"They learned what they needed to."

"Which is?"

Voss's eyes stayed on the moving truck.

"How much they can get away with."

Cole shook his head once.

Behind them, a press briefing started. Voices amplified, controlled, practiced.

"…no ongoing threat to surrounding regions…"

"…park closure remains temporary…"

"…visitor safety remains our highest priority…"

Cole turned away from it.

Didn't need to hear the rest.

Voss adjusted his glasses, gaze fixed somewhere beyond the visible damage—farther out, where the system ran deeper than anyone wanted to admit.

"You were right," he said.

Cole didn't look at him.

"Yeah."

"It's not stable."

"No."

Voss nodded once, slowly.

The admission cost him something.

Cole could see it.

Feel it.

A low tremor rolled through the ground.

Subtle.

Cole felt it.

Voss did too.

Neither of them spoke.

The helicopters kept moving.

The officials kept talking.

The story kept shifting into something easier to accept.

Cole stared out over what was left of Yellowstone.

Then beyond it.

Because this wasn't finished.

"This was only contained," he said quietly.

Voss didn't correct him.

Not stopped.

Beneath his boots, the ground shifted again—just enough to feel.

www.ingramcontent.com/pod-product-compliance
Lightning Source LLC
LaVergne TN
LVHW090954080826
845145LV00003B/1006

* 9 7 8 1 9 7 1 0 6 0 3 1 6 *